LONDON INDEPENDENT STORY PRIZE 2024

SHORT STORY WINNERS & FINALISTS

ANTHOLOGY

First published in Great Britain
by the London Independent Story Prize, 2025
e.info: entry@londonindependentstoryprize.co.uk
www.londonindependentstoryprize.co.uk
Follow us on Twitter and Instagram @Londonisp
www.facebook.com/LIStoryPrize

978-1-7384671-9-8
British Library Cataloguing-in-Publication Data
A catalogue record of this book is available from
the British Library.
Cover art by Demet Okyar Ceyhan

LONDON
INDEPENDENT
STORY PRIZE

Table of Contents

Introduction

London Independent Story Prize (LISP) is a Community Interest Company founded by storytellers for storytellers. LISP aims to nurture brave voices and create sustainable networking opportunities for writers and filmmakers. Our purpose is to build a community that embraces multicultural differences, bold voices, unique writers, and extraordinary artistic approaches to storytelling.

The stories compiled in this anthology were selected from the LISP 2024 competition. Aligning with LISP's core strategies, these stories are not edited or polished by professional editors and proofreaders. We acknowledge that language skills, such as grammar and spelling, are linked to access to education. Therefore, LISP does not seek excellence in those elements but values the distinct voice of the writer, the originality of the stories and braveness in the storytelling techniques the most. Enjoy reading these fantastic stories.

London Independent Story Prize 1st Round Winner

Alice Frecknall

Baby, I know

When she comes she has me in a headlock fist-stopping her own mouth, soft chest to soft chest. I tell her I want to die. I want to die, I say. Meaning, I love you. Meaning, leave your wife for me. The next day, I send photos of pigeons to her phone instead of wish you were here thinking of you miss you I feel like a gnarled bird. We meet for dinner and neither of us mentions the pigeons. The waiter takes our order says allergies with a question mark and I shake my head whilst looking firm across the table. Meaning, don't let me consume her. Not a taste. Another taste. I can barely eat a thing, but I like to watch as she goes between the dishes we agreed to share. My stomach fills. I want to die I want to die I want to die. I want to die, I tell her. But she's not getting it. I want to die I love you. It's easy, see. I want to die, I say. Meaning, I love you. Make this stop, I mean. We watch a movie and I try to focus. Screen/ ceiling/ original M&Ms. Stain my tongue dirty sky let her kiss me. She takes her top off and her ribs are perfect. We go to bed and when she comes she has me in a headlock. Under my breath is the most daring I can be. I want to die, I whisper. You could say I'm addicted: screen/ ceiling/ original M&Ms/ the scent of her. Let's go to Paris, I say. Why not Amsterdam, the moon, anywhere. Can we? Please. Just to see what we look like in another place. Without gravity holding us down I think things would be different. I think if we got high or walked to the top of a high building or jumped off the top of a very high building. I want to die, I tell her. Meaning, I'm in love with you. Meaning, leave your wife for me. The two of them are in a frame on the bookshelf. The bedlinen smells of sleep and skin. None of it mine. I tell her my ex liked the idea of me but that's as far as we got. Between the hours of 3 and 5am, I dream I am drowning and it's glorious. Stand on my sternum, I yell into her ear before her eyes are even open. Jump on my sternum here's my nipple take these scissors, I dare you. Here's my nipple I dare you do you dare me. I want to die, I say, let me prove it. She looks me in the face like I'm a picture of madness. You won't do me this favour? I say, this tiny little favour. Won't you pinch me, get your nails out, not even? Don't you want a piece of me, a little keepsake don't you owe me a little physical pain make your mark on me. A week passes and neither of us mentions my nipples. At the birthday picnic of a mutual friend, I'm a messy secret. My hair is having a bad day. Every bit of me is having a bad day. She goes round two on a potato salad sent with apologies from her wife. At the birthday picnic everyone loves her. Have you met her? they say. The wife. Such a sweetheart such a pure heart (such a kink) a busy bee have you met, my god you must simply must. You'll love her, they say, they just know, how could anyone not. How could anyone. I eat half an egg hardboiled, hope to choke don't chew, soft push of throat and swallow. Someone's left a baby on the floor. Crawling around on the floor. A baby with tiny toes under my hard heel. Now it's a party. A baby on the floor screaming red faced snotty lipped purple pain. I didn't see her I'm sorry, I say. Tell me about it, baby, I say. Baby, I know. Sweep her up such a sweetheart such a pure heart snotty faced red lipped. I'm so sorry, I didn't see. Purple screaming snotty red I did. Tell me about it baby I did baby I know. I know.

Her wife returns from a trip out of town and it's silence. Twenty-four degrees, fancy a dip? Picture of a cat. No reply. Fifty percent chance of precipitation won't you meet me?

Picture of a shadow a duck a sunset. No reply it's silence.
For five days silence and counting. I look for her on the
Internet and when I come it's to a photo of her wife
somewhere hot, tattooed thighs sweating glass the clichés.
A whole week of silence, then she breaks. We meet for
coffee in a café that's more animals than people. She
empties a sachet of brown sugar, watches it sink, takes a
spoon and stirs, points out a corgi a dachshund. I smile then
silence, for five minutes silence and counting. I pick up my
cup put it down, I missed you. She reaches across the table
and for a second we're holy. Two hours pass. By the time
we're done I feel like a puppet. I'm broke but pick up the
bill. In the street we hold each other, don't kiss. Over her
shoulder: traffic/ sky/ newsagent's/ the scent of her/ you'll
never leave your wife for me. We go to bed and she fakes it,
I refuse. Morning and she tops me with whatever's to hand.
Bottle neck/ Berocca tube. Morning and I let her. I want to
die, I tell her. Meaning, I'm in love with you. I want to die
won't you let me. I touch her and she fakes it, I refuse. She
holds me, tells me baby, I know. I know. She leaves the
room. I finish what she started. Bottle neck/ Berocca tube.
On the other side of the wall the sound of the shower, her
body the slip of her body perfect ribs. I make breakfast,
avoid eggs, cold toast buttered tea. Her wife keeps their fruit
bowl well-stocked. I force my thumb through a kiwi get my
nails out, pierce skin find core, turn it over let the flies in.
Wet haired, she finds me sobbing on the tiles, vomit in the
sink. She looks at me and her eyes are magnificent. Tell me
about it, baby, she says. Meaning, please don't. Meaning my
god what's wrong with you? She looks at me and I think,
you could end me could I end you, let her kiss me. The next
day, I send memes to her phone instead of sorry I can't let's
be serious get real. I leave my brain off the hook, walk to
the river and strip. Clothes to the ground tangled skin, tide
out and sandy. A girl skims stones on the water. She stands

4

with her back to me, one two three gone one two three. It's easy, I say, if you pick such a smooth one, don't you want a challenge a real challenge. She turns and her jaw is a teenager, tries not to look keep her eyes up she's staring. Have a go, she says, holds out a hand and her wrists are perfect. I take it. Pebble flat to my palm warmth of her grip, watch it throw for a second then gone, slip of smooth body swallowed down. She's laughing. From behind my bare shoulder happy-faced and laughing, the water licks at my ankles, soft backs of my knees. I push out. Come in, I say, why don't you? Just for a moment it's painful. But she's staring and not, and walking and gone. I float stomach up, back of my head in an ice bath. I think of the wife, her wife, and my hands start to purple, shrivelled fingertips. Stagger out against the drag, pull my clothes on still wet check my phone: tired selfie no words. The arc of her eyebrow is a question. I take a photo of the incoming dusk, caption it: my hollowed-out chest. Delete. Caption it: I miss you/ caption: it hurts/ make it stop/ leave me alone/ don't stop/ don't/ leave me I beg you won't beg you delete. LOOK! the sky showed up heart eyes, press send. I head home along the foreshore don't get there. Take a right, over the bridge turn the corner. The living room window flickers with a game show, car kerbside hot rubber the sound of shrinking metal.

London Independent Story Prize 2nd Round Winner

Han Smith

Syzygy

Look up but the birds are higher, somewhere. Here are our feet on the bed of the sea.

I know I'm not quite ocean now because that's what's slipping away as we stand. It drains and is final past heels and is creeping out to be horizon. What's left is to know that I wanted this: this is where I chose to come, and wait. Look up, and this is the distance you are. You said I'd never see anything like this place.

We watch and when circles take shape in the sediment, the figure that is Matze kicks clod grains from the pitchfork. He shrugs and says they're not to scale. But he says we can guess what he's drawn with the metal. One's the sun and one's the moon and in between there's a blunted Earth.
I know, says one of the group. It's showing how the tides are made, she says.
Matze nods to say she's right. An ear appears on the side of the Earth when he lifts the fork again and says, The water on our planet being pulled towards the moon. He pokes a hole where the lobe meets Earth. And that's a place it's low tide, like where we are now, he says. But when the Earth spins further round like it does all the time, that place will be in the middle of

where the water's pulled high by the moon, he says, and there's a mark again in the sand to prove it.
He says the sea-bulge sticking out keeps where it is because the moon stays more or less just there when only part of the day is gone. And then when the hole is under the bulge, the tide is high and covers things.
There's spring and neap as well, he says, but now there are too many lines in the sand, and the thickness of the surface is sucking down the joints. Matze says it is time to move on. It's time to dig for crabs and worms further out.

When we're wading through where the water's still deep, a woman stops ahead of me while Matze walks on. We used to come here every year, she says. We used to come here every spring and again in the autumn, just like the geese.
On the other side, across the creek, she leaves prints with her boots that swallow away. She says she knows this place like her hands and she shows me, with one of them out of its glove and then the other, and the backs of them really are maps, or stripped brains.
She says that sunset when the tide is in is physical and raging and close against skin. A low-water sunset is vast but untouchable, paled-through pink in scattered reflection only where the puddles still sit. But it's never the same and there's everything in between to look for as well, she says.

We level with Matze and he plunges the fork. The inside is wet and moves with veins, and he knows the names and lists them for us. There are thick black worms that cast trails like their bodies, and flatter ones in brighter colours and fringes ribboned along each side. The smallest are fragile in red and stretched taut. I watch because I have to know too. I follow when he gives his tours for the people that come, by ferry when the sea is deep enough or in horse-drawn carts across the mud when it's bared.

I'll read through his notes in a cardboard folder. I'll have to learn the outlines to draw by their feet, and where to find starfish, where to find amber, and the direction for wrecks on the clearest days. Matze can't be the only one so I'll hold the pitchfork when he needs to rest. His shadow in a dark room is nothing like yours. I'll carve the likeness of the moon and the sun and give my own words to try to explain.

You have to let it go, says the woman in the ebb. You have to let it go and then you have to let it back.

And this is where we chose to be. This was your promise before it seeped dry.

*

When you told me about your grandfather Jens, you told me that he was the last of the pirates. His uncles and brothers denied it all their lives, but when only Jens was left he snapped his pipe into its box one evening and told you all it was true, you said.

No one from outside or the mainland ever came here in those days on purpose, you said. There were four families and four farms like there had been for years. There was a windmill and there were storms and sometimes floods that tore in. They built the dike and

8

kept it strong with clay but it wasn't always firm enough, and they drove stakes into the mud when the water was out that spread in rays away from the land. They wove brushwood between them so that sand and other singled fragments would catch and mount slowly, until salt-grass would grow. They wanted more space for the cattle and sheep.

So this was one way they redrew the shoreline, and the other one was what made them pirates. It happens wherever the edges can be played with. Here, they made use of the suddenness of retreat: the calamitous and inevitable voiding by the tide.

It could be arranged in advance if they knew that something they wanted or needed was due to pass by, and in this case they set up lanterns in planned patterns. The boats then stuck because the depths were wrong. While the women acted panic and offered up blankets, the men and older boys stole back to the night and saw their hands take up the rewards they had pictured in their minds already.

But there were also the spontaneous raids, you said. Instead of anticipating alignments and making steady preparations, a minute flash from a vessel's metal parts would reveal that it had listed off-course. Or the wind with its own unknown persuasions would take an unexpected role, or rainfall or lack of it would shift the sand shelves. These were the real conquests, unpredicted: there was a rush of lamps, of leather gloves, of flame and crates and waterlogged boots. The wares they recovered on nights like this were never as immediately practical as the shipments they had time to plot to divert, but they had a different gleam of unlikeliness. The adventure was more special, and bolder.

The word for island, in what your grandfather spoke, was Oie or just O, you said. I remembered this because it seemed so lone.

But you said we'd be together there.

*

In winter, the boats and the tourists stop. Instead the motion is the restlessness of every way the sea has found to freeze. The first time, there are fingers of ice between the sand ribs, and when the water comes in and out over hours, the finger ends join to make a sheet-crust that is smooth. Then it's thicker and the plates of it break, and meld back together at shifted angles. On days that are warmer, the flood makes them loosen. What used to be solid is weakened slowly, and feet sink through twice, through the buttered surface above once ice and then through the usual gulped sand beneath. It's layers of things and what can be covered. But we have to think of how to use this winter, before the boats start coming again. I paint birds from books to remember them: paint them into pale insides of shells and colour the edges for an oval frame. The edges are where each shell became half, and I paint each half a different bird.

When it doesn't rain, we have the nature-trail to check on, with its numbered panels in a loop around the island. We unscrew the glass and pages are wet and we change them but never alter the texts. One is the panel at the start of the East Foreland, where the ground nests will be and there are rules for the paths. Others show lichens, or the difference of seasons.

By the visitors' centre, where the trail ends, the photograph is bones and ripped plumage and a ribcage, full of gritted orange coils and netting. Next to it is a clear box, of similarly twisted pieces but there are more of them and they are larger. The words here say that this is how much plastic was found inside the stomach of the tern in the photo, proportional to a human's size. You can spin a cube to see four different plots of the coastline from each of the last four centuries. Points are made by stretching scales and shrinking them. How many times have I walked the loop now? Sometimes we stalk the driftline for more torn wings, and debris.

A letter came for you, says Matze. Matze's fingertips towards me are nothing like yours. Is this the one you've been waiting for? he says.

There is a graveyard behind the visitors' centre and this graveyard has a name. The graveyard's name is the Graveyard of the Nameless. Seventeen bodies under seventeen crosses are here because this is where the sea has left them.

This is where I open the envelope. The envelope holds a name but no body.

*

Boats never stray off course there now, you said. They have their routes on machines and dials and these can warn them when something looks wrong. No one tries to claim land from the sea these days either, because they don't even have the animals to fill it. There are beds, an inn, and rides out in carriages instead, all for curiosity and visitors. They depend on the outside completely now and the strange thing is the tourists only come because it's not part of everything else, you said.

My grandfather Jens was the last, you said. It won't ever be that way again. He even used to bury what he took, like treasure.

This now is a time of freezing and breakage, of polyethylene, polypropylene, and polyvinyl chloride. Polystyrene, polyurethane, polyethylene terephthalate, and pieces travel in the rarest ways to places they don't belong.

*

When spring sets in, the geese come back, and so does the woman who remembered the sunsets. It's never quite the same, she says again. It can make you feel certain of one moment in time, or it tells you that you're everything forever.

And when the tide comes in, I remember, too. You said I'd never see beauty like this place, a world that grows and shrinks with the sea. You told me that you needed to wait and be sure. You said we had to get away. You knew somewhere we could go: the island where your grandparents were born. You said they took on people in pairs to give tours, that there was a bedroom and a kitchen at the bottom of the lighthouse. The sea all around slides back with the ebb, you said. You can walk on the seabed for miles and miles but you have to know when to turn back, or you'll drown.

So here: this landscape of mud and forgetting. Here: the planet I mark in the sand, and here: where nature is shown in pictures. I'm in the pair that gives the tours, and you're a name on a postcard, an apology in three lines. Matze's shadow on the wash margin is nothing like yours.

When the tide comes in, half-things are almost whole, for as long as they can be, until it leaves as it comes. It washes out our attempts to draw the forces of the universe. Let it go, and let it come back. The driftline is never not a seam sewn of haunting.

London Independent Story Prize 1st Round Winner

Mary Ethna Black

The Thaw

The *before* of Arabella Denton's journey was laid out in a predictable way, while the *after* holds, deliberately, no shape at all. In between is that trip north to where the black pines of an Alaskan forest punch through Styrofoam snow. The forces of the passing seasons and the brutal winter weather batters those trees, yet they cling on until spring arrives, patches of the permafrost melt, and the iron grip of the frozen earth loosens. In summer, they lean over by degrees until winter returns to brace their roots once more in place, each one crooked. And every so often, one falls.

*

Arabella Denton sits against a tree at the edge of the clearing. The old pine has a rough surface pitted with nooks and crannies; no bugs crawl over it in this dead of winter. It is as if this tree has been expecting her arrival, and they have formed a bond, human back to tough bark. A familiar sound, that plink as she opens the screw cap on her bottle of bourbon. She takes a swig.

A rustle in a pile of fallen branches makes Arabella start, but it's probably some small creature, scratching out a living, nothing more. Her gaze follows the smudged line of her fast-filling footprints back to the edge of the trail, where her snowmobile glows a

14

metallic orange. After she turned off the motor, she had expected silence in the forest, but no—there is a constant clicking, tiny snaps. The conversation of frozen trees.

'Let's go to Alaska,' George said after his diagnosis. He showed her the New York Times travel supplement about the Northern Lights, turned the page to show her a ripple of purple across a dark sky, traced the swell as it soared over the forest. His finger traveled on, following the curve of treetops to the edge of the page, on across the dining room table, tracing the wood grain beneath layers and years of varnish, all the way to where her hand was waiting. There was a light in his eyes as he took it. She knew what George was thinking: you and me, for one last adventure.

'I'm not done yet, Arabella. Please. Melanie will be fine.'

Squeezing the familiar warm palm, she nodded. 'She's all grown up now, doesn't need us.'

*

This forest conveys the natural reverence of a cathedral. With each passing year, another aged trunk quits the congregation, leaving a wooden corpse to lie unevenly here and there. The upright trees waver as if they are praying. A candle would be lovely, thinks Arabella, I can wave it around like they do at rock concerts. A pinpoint of light, a little blessing on this place. Has she brought matches? No, of course not.

'Listen to this, Arabella,' said George. 'When the old, sick Inuit know their time is up, they walk deep into the winter forest and wait beside a tree. They fall asleep and freeze to death. It's painless, a good way to go.'

'Is that real, or did you see it in a movie, dear?'

He closed his eyes as if he was fishing for a memory, trying to pull it clear of a tangle in his marshy thoughts. But no, it was all gone.

'I don't know.'

Arabella searched online and found a true life account. An ailing elder from Fairbanks had set out to die, but her city-bred family panicked and sent out a search party to bring the old woman home. Once more, the woman evaded her loved ones, once more they rescued her. Settled into a nursing home behind a securely locked door, the old woman took to her bed and turned away from all activities until, eventually, she died.

Poor George grew ever more confused, cooped up in that nursing home, unkempt, not always clean, sullen at times. When he no longer recognized her or Melanie, it was too late for a trip to see the Aurora Borealis, so they watched the Discovery Channel instead, the Alaskan wilderness confined now within the square window of the screen. Then one day, George was gone.

*

Another morning, another cup of coffee, another solo breakfast. The forest green Birkin bag waited, neatly packed—Chanel Rouge Coco Flash lipstick, iPad in

16

leather case, iPhone ditto, Smythson notebook, Mont Blanc fountain pen with sepia ink—today she wasn't going anywhere, calendar empty, not even a lunch engagement. If she stretched it out, breakfast and the New York Times could fill a good hour before, well, before what?

Arabella let her gaze follow the line of her curated oil paintings, pink peonies in bowls, cream linen sofa. Family photos in filigree frames clustered on top of the piano. Melanie in Guipure lace, throwing her bouquet of white roses. Melanie graduating from Princeton with two proud parents: George in that awful tweed suit, too warm for the day, she had warned him. Her favourite photo, taken on the steps of St Patrick's Cathedral on 5th Avenue. All three wrapped up against the wind before midnight mass. The choir had sung all her favourites. *Silent night, holy night, all is calm, all is bright. In the Bleak mid-winter...snow had fallen snow on snow, snow on snow. Oh little Star of Bethlehem, how still we see thee lie.* They would light candles before the side altar to St Christopher, patron saint of travellers. *Protect me today in all my travels along the road's way... Be at my window and direct me through when vision blurs... Carry me safely to my destined place...*

Melanie as a Christmas angel aged seven. Hours of work, those wings had taken to make. Blobs of PVA glue on the table, fragmenets of white crepe paper scattered across the carpet like snow.

With a silver spoon Arabella stirred her coffee, took a sip and sets the cup down on a placemat: there was no point in ruining the French polish on her

Georgian table. The worried look on the internist's face as he formed the first sentence. We've got your biopsy results and the tumor markers... fairly treatable with these experimental drugs... worth a shot. The neat plan for how she might claw back another few years. He omitted to say this: after all that fuss and expense, you will end your days wasting away in a hospice. Just like George. Possibly with a colostomy bag, or in adult nappies. Melanie wiping her bottom, awful thought. And the pain, there would be pain.

Arabella pushed the ends of her grey bob behind her ear, drank her coffee, and opened the Times. Having flipped through the news section, she shuffled the inserts and out fell a travel brochure. See the world. Venice dwarfed by a monstrous cruise ship. Hong Kong harbour with skyscrapers and sampans. Alaska: huskies and sleds, a cruise ship dwarfed by a fjord. Trip of a lifetime, the magnificent Northern Lights. George. Oh—

And there it was: the moment of dissolution. What if I go now? I could set off to the unknown, to the north. An adventure, with no preparation and not much of a plan. Just head into a forest to sit by a tree, wait for the Northern Lights and go out beneath a blaze of glory. One last hurrah. Now that has a ring to it, a glow.

Her iPhone rang. Melanie calling.

...

'Yes Melanie, I'm enthusiastic about the chemo.'

...

'I'm fine, having a nice cup of coffee.'

18

...

'I might go away for a short trip, take a cruise before the next round.'

...

'I'm sure they do have a doctor on board.'

...

'All-inclusive, but I won't take the optional drinks package, so you don't need to worry. I won't fall overboard.'

*

In the drunken forest, the ignition key, flung far, is buried in a drift. Wolves will come, but hopefully later, after her heart has stopped beating. St Christopher has his wooden staff at the ready. He'll bonk them on the nose.

'Came all the way up here for—. Saw it in the brochure. Forgotten the name of that thing. George said—'

Arabella has an unexpected flash of something like regret, but she pushes that emotion to the back of her mind. There is a small, warm hand in hers and a childish voice: something about snowflakes and Christmas, a frail thread that barely holds. Branches creak under the weight of snow; every tiny sound amplified, as if the tree is conversing back.

'Do hurry up, Northern Lights. Appear. And who on earth am I telling this to, eh? A tree?'

The branches shift, and there is that small hand in hers again. Fleeting.

'This is not the stuff I—not how I want her to remember me: her mother a dead drunk.'

On cue, the empty bottle drops from her numb fingers and the neck peeks out of a drift.

'Don't want them to find this when they dig me out in the spring. God, no, that's just awful. Must bury it deeper.'

As she reaches towards the bottle, Arabella topples sideways and can't get up, so she curls back against the rough trunk. The snow falls, as if God is wielding a giant rubber to soften all the lines. Eventually, white will cover everything and erase her. With the buzz from the bourbon, drifting off is pleasant. They will find her in springtime, with the thaw.

A burning sensation jolts her awake. Amidst the snow-covered humps of fallen trees, Arabella is aflame. Fire rips through her legs and arms, heat surges through her chest. As she fumbles for the zip of her parka, a faint singing beckons from the sky. Arabella gazes up as ribbons of colour billow across the ink black sky. Too hot, much too hot. She knows what this is. Paradoxical undressing, when you are in the last stages of hypothermia and shed your clothes, burning up. Or is it joy? Purple, green, lilac, the bands move in a sedate swirl, enfolding the pin-pricks of the stars, banishing all cold.

'I love this.' she cries, as colors fill her vision. 'I hear you. You have a song, like tiny bells.'

With arms outstretched, fully alive, Arabella dances, dances, until the ground tips her over and she falls and the snowflakes drift softly around her. There is another sound in the air, the mechanical grind of approaching snowmobiles. Perhaps not, it's hard to tell.

*

Someone is talking. Why? The tone is warm, and the voice penetrates muffled background sounds until the words melt together to form phrases.

'... and when you get out of here... live with us... of course it'll be a great help with the new baby, and... we'd love to have you...'

She recognizes that voice: Melanie. What on earth is her daughter doing here in the forest? The words swell and fade, as if the volume is being turned up and down, letting through the odd fragment. Arabella wants to interject—I don't want anyone to find me—but she can't raise the energy.

'Did you hear, Mom? I'm pregnant.'

'That's very nice,' says Arabella, her voice faint. Nice will do well enough. Nothing complicated is required, just enough to be left alone again. If only she could think of something more profound. Melanie will make a wonderful mother with those lovely big white angel wings. Took ages to make them. All that crepe paper. No, something else. It must be snow.

Arabella extracts her hand and raises stiff fingers in the air to follow the dance of the falling flakes.

'What were those lines...'

'Mom?'

'I remember now. A feathered morsel sifts through white. Ghosts of centimes falling. In flocks and flurry.'

'That poem of mine wasn't very good,' says Melanie.

'It was pretty terrific for a ten-year-old.'

Arabella is awake now. She touches the wrinkle on her daughter's forehead, a permanent furrow. How had that happened?

'The poem was perfect. Like you.'

'Please don't go yet, Mom. stay a while longer.'

Arabella searches for the right words. 'Can you catch a snowflake for me?'

'I can't hold the flakes. They're melting.'

Arabella reaches towards her daughter's hand. As their living skin connects, the distance between them fills with meltwater.

*

All through that winter, Arabella's tree stands witness as small creatures and birds come and go, leaving fine tracks in the crooked aisles of the snow-bound forest. The forest is rough and almost silent, and a strange light that you can see and feel glows through the night and will set you ablaze. Every so often, the Aurora Borealis murmurs an incantation. The arboreal choir replies in its own way: the trunks make low sounds, snow whispers on loaded branches, and icicles crackle. As spring nears, the intermittent permafrost, for it is not a solid thing as many believe, relaxes its grip here and there, allowing the tree to lean over a little more.

Out there, way up North, where stars are the streetlights, and the Aurora sings, some say that a tree waits for each and every one of us.

London Independent Story Prize 1st Round Finalist

Fiona Dignan

A Woman of Substance

My mother was a wet weather woman. That is why she and I were born still encased in our cauls; we couldn't bear to be parted from the waters. I am named for the goddess Satyavati who is called a *Matsyakanya* because she was born from the womb of a fish. Throughout my childhood, I would check to see if my limbs were sprouting scales, disappointed when they remained stubbornly skin. I waited for my true mermaid form to emerge.

*****

As a young child, I loved to watch my mother standing naked amongst the banyan trees, whenever the rains came. She taught me the names of all the different types of waters – *ṭhīk* for the rains that came slight as a strand of hair. *Bhari* for the jewels of heavy drizzle that rose over the Western Ghat mountains and covered the village like a blanket of diamonds. *Chaoukala* for the monsoon rains that came signalled by cauliflower towers of clouds. And the legendary *him*, the rain that turned to white feathers and lay atop of the mountains. She taught me the pitter-patter sound of raindrops striking the surface of the earth is produced by bubbles

24

of air wavering underwater. She and I would dance barefoot to the beat of the air wavering, coating our toes in the glutinous mud.

When I was still a girl, our favourite game was jumping in puddles large as lakes when the rainy season came. We always remained barefoot, wanting the water to soak between the crevices of our toes, watching the puddles fill and rise up our legs like silk stockings. The blue pansy and crimson rose butterflies would come to drink in the puddles. The confetti of their wings settled as they landed by our feet.

"Look," my mother would say, "even the creatures of the air must come down to the waters. Water is the primary essence."

***

By the time I started school, I began to notice things about my mother. Or rather, how other people noticed her. The women of the village would snigger into their saris when she bought her herbs from the market. At the golden temple, villagers kept their distance. Once the local boys caught pink perch and threw them into our fig tree. We didn't find them until the next afternoon when the smell of putrid flesh blew across us. My mother picked the perch from the tree with delicacy and buried the fish under the sacred peepal tree. I stood and watched her on our porch, feeling a thing of two halves. Part of me felt pity for the fish, and my mother gathering them into their grave. Yet part of me felt ashamed of how she drew the boys' attention with her ways. I was at the age where I noticed, the other women and girls did not act like us.

I tried to become a child of the land like my classmates. A child who longed for the solidity of the dry earth beneath her feet. I started to enjoy those hazy summer days of lying in the wildflower meadows with the other girls, making chains of marigolds into necklaces. I felt like I had the sun around my neck. I found places where I could stay dry and normal. My mother would call to me when the rains came, but I ignored her pleas and I watched her from my window, reddened with embarrassment at her scaly, rain beaten body.

As I grew more landbound my skin began to itch, then peel. I slathered sheens of ghee onto my sores but I secretly craved the rain. I wanted that sublime feeling of standing under a darkening monsoon sky as it burst. But I was growing up and needed to ignore such childish desires.

My skin continued to itch until it bled. As it healed it grew back glittered and silvered. I wrapped bandages over my arms in shame, hid under dresses with long silk sleeves. I kept away from puddles and rains and rivers and even the village pump. I was fearful of the water talking to my body, calling it into its elemental form.

By the time I started my first bleed, my mother would soak herself for hours in the old cow trough she filled with water from the river. I looked at her in her true form, the magnificence of sequins of scales and felt only repulsion. The wetness reminded me of the flood of blood seeping out of me. I did not want this transformation. I did not want to become my strange and unaccepted mother. I wanted to change my essence.

***

The ancient woman ,Aaji Saraswati, lived deep inside the forest below the mountain. Her fame for alchemy was known throughout the seven villages, but a woman with the power to alter substance was not someone you visited lightly. I walked for half a day through the bush to find her shack, hidden by bamboo and startling purple rhododendrons.

I knocked and upon opening the door saw a crumpled woman sitting on her reed chatai. Her eyes were milky as chai, her face etched like the cracked earth and her gums caved in, toothless.

"Satyavati child, why do you come to me?" she asked in the voice of a much younger woman.

"I am a child of the water." I told her. "I want to be a child of the land."

She sucked her gums together, rose and waddled to her cabinet and drew a jar of red sand.

"Once, many years ago, when I was just a child, the winds swept up the desert sands and brought red rain to our village. It was as though the sky was bleeding. Swallow this my child if you truly wish to change what you are. But transforming is a great sin, and a price must be paid to the gods you offend."

I crossed her palm with a silver coin and ran out into the forest. Beneath the canopy of green I tipped the sand into my mouth. It scratched and clogged in my throat, I retched and writhed on the forest floor, but I swallowed it down. I could feel it clumping in my stomach, whirring like a desert storm inside me. I was unsure if it was guilt or wonder I felt.

Over the following weeks I bathed out in the heat of the midday sun, my skin smooth and brown. I picked lotus blooms with the village girls and let the butcher's boy touch my secret places with his clammy hands. My mother receded into the background of my life as I became landlocked. One day, she gazed at my skin and told me,

"You have broken your caul."

**

When the monsoon rains came that year, my mother asked me to come jump,

"One last time?" she pleaded. "Soon you will be a woman with a home of your own." But I refused, the thought of all that dampness touching my skin filled me with an indescribable horror.

From our front porch I watched her strip her clothes off, revealing her silvered skin and she jumped from puddle to puddle until she fell into one that swallowed her whole. I ran from the porch, felt into the water with my hands but felt nothing but the shallow mud beneath. My mother had gone beyond to the underworld of waters where the fish and mermaids lived. I could not follow now, I was a creature of the land.

***

For months I searched for my mother in every body of water I could find, in the Pravara River, the Tringalwadi Lake, the temple stream. I even looked in the small dribbles left by the village pump, in my glass, in the trough in the garden. Occasionally I would glimpse a flit of quicksilver out of the corner of my eye. But my mother remained elusive.

As the rains gave way to the relentless heat, the streams and puddles dried. The land became cracked and hard. The following year, the monsoon rains failed to come and the pink perch lay lifeless on the riverbed.

That year, I was married to the butcher's boy and became a true woman of the land. I lay still and silent as his blood-stained hands would reach towards me in the fever of the night. I had offended the gods and my price was paid. When my bloods failed to show the following month and the smells of the morning idli made me vomit, I knew my child must be born of the water.

I trekked back through the forest, hot and nauseous, to find Aaji Saraswati's shack. Her door was already open and she sat on her reed mat with her blind eyes fixed on me.

"Satyavati, I have waited for you these many years."

"Then you know what I come to ask you for auntie?"

"Of course, but I told you, you would pay your price for offending the gods."

"But my child should not be punished for my sins. I must become a child of the water again. I am parched in this desolate dryness and my child, I know she will die in this heat."

"That is in the hands of the gods my child. I can't transform a substance back again."

"There must be some way? Please auntie, I have paid my price."

"Tell me child, why did you wish to change your essence?"

I was caught off guard by the direct question but answered as truthfully as I knew,

"I was afraid, I was afraid of becoming my mother. I was afraid of the names the villagers called her."

"Ah yes, fear," chuckled Aaji Saraswati, "you have learnt that fear is just the substance of love turned inside out."

I was unsure of the riddles the old woman spoke of.

"Yes, I should have never feared becoming what I loved. But how can that help me now?"

"Change is a one-way process, until it comes to love. That has an alchemy all of its own. Go back home child, pray to the goddess whose name you bear and wait for the rain. When the monsoon returns, you shall have your daughter."

***

I went straight to the golden temple and prayed to the goddess. I sought out every drop of dew I could find on the lotus flowers, dug my fingers deep into the riverbed until a slight smear of mud appeared.

My child continued to grow and by the time the skin on my belly had swollen taut, the towering clouds appeared over the mountains. When the first rains came, my body buckled under the vice of contractions. I lay amongst the banyan trees as the storm burst over me and screamed into the power of the goddess and my mother. My daughter was born in her caul and I broke her waters to heave her raw newborn body against my breast. I named her Paani after my mother and after our essence – water.

***

Now Paani is a young child and my body has grown back silver where she stretched my skin. And I teach her the names of all the types of rains. When the monsoon comes, we jump barefoot into the puddles and swim in the swollen belly of the lake. I teach her all my mother taught me and tell her she must never become something she is not. I no longer care what my husband or the villagers say of me. I have lost my mother and there is no greater pain they can inflict with their dry gossipy mouths.

As the monsoon eases, I take Paani and show her the spot in the forest where the butterflies come to drink. We lie on our bellies and peer carefully into the pool as to not disturb the delicate blue and pink wings. And just for a moment, I catch a swish of silver in the pool and the face of my mother is reflected back up at me.

London Independent Story Prize 1st Round Finalist

Katy Severson

Dear Julia (London Fields)

Dear Julia,

The days are long without you, but I'll say I'm never bored — how could I be? With all the thousands of stories unfolding around me. Here in London Fields on a Sunday, I'm watching two crows hunt a mouse and pick it apart and all the while a London Plane lost three leaves and I caught each one glimmering in the low afternoon light, drifting toward the ground like a parachute. A couple in wool coats is carrying a Christmas tree wrapped in white wiry mesh, and they're arguing about whether to put it in the bay window or closer to the entrance, and you have to wonder what the trees think about all this: people dragging little severed beings across the park and up stairwells into flats where we decorate them with tinsel and ornaments and little flashing lights and then place gifts around the bottom like an altar. Do you think Christmas is a time of mourning for the trees? One of the big ones lining the pedestrian path has two lumps on its trunk that look just like a furrowed brow. And I know if you were here, we'd giggle about that for at least another hour until one of our stomachs rumbled and we'd go off to the pub around the corner and order sticky pudding and you'd tell me all about the fungal networks under the soil and the messages they send each other. The dogs are the only ones who seem to notice the trees. I love to watch them galloping through piles of fallen leaves with the most gleeful little looks on their faces, drool hanging off their whiskers. There are two dogs right now chasing each other — a white one with pointy ears too big for its head and a larger curly one the colour of a double-crust apple pie when you've used plenty of egg wash. You'd love that one. Sunlight flickers through the horse chestnut tree at the West end of the park and a conker falls, and then another. It's all quite lovely. I'm sitting on a bench by Broadway Market now and there's a man across the road adding charcoal to a barbecue, fingers caked in soot and one shoe untied, and you have to wonder how long it's been like that and if maybe he has something heavy on his mind and that's why he's forgotten — or perhaps he has a crush on someone and he's thinking about touching their scalp with his fingers and the perfume of their hair and what kind of soup he might make for them to eat naked over the stove after having sex all afternoon. And in the midst of all that wondering, two birds swoop in and land on the bench beside me. I think they're starlings as they have the little white polka dots on their little black bellies, and one sings a little song — more guttural than melodic. Did you know, Julia, that the Blitz nearly obliterated London Fields? Well not the park but all the homes around it, massive fires lit the night and people fled to tube stations for shelter from the bombs. Strange to think the trees have seen it all. They've seen the war, the crime, the gentrification. And surely they've seen love. Teens making out against their trunks. Men bouncing babies on their shoulders. I've just looked across the way and seen a woman through the window of a flat above the off-license dancing with a little girl. And then the smell of curry wafted by, and it reminds me that we never went to India like we said we would. I'd rather not go without you, but I will if I must. And two planes are flying above, crisscrossing in the sky, which always blows my mind a bit. Each one full of hundreds of people all with their own reasons to be off somewhere. Isn't it funny to think that while they're soaring

34

through the sky, a woman in a neck scarf is probably offering them something to drink — and maybe someone is buying a beer for their neighbour, and a kid is ripping open a packet of crisps, and a man on his way to a funeral is buying two gins, one to drink with tonic, and one in his pocket for later? I think I'll bake bread when I get home. I bought a few potatoes at the market and some nice salted butter and a new friend of mine, Max, gave me a little bit of his sourdough starter last week and he said if I feed it with rye flour it does best. So I've been feeding it for 3 days and I do think it's ready and I'll keep in mind what you said when we first made a loaf together, in that room lit by the woodstove, orange light flickering in the foggy windows, *Don't be afraid of the bread, it senses your fear,* and I'll try to approach it all with confidence. Oh Julia, now a man's just walked by with a leek in his tote and it reminds me of all those wild leeks you showed me on the Cornish coast, snacking on their little white flowers, salty from the sea breeze. And of course the fish & chips we ate that night, tearing greasy hunks of cod from the brown paper bag, our oily fingers intertwined over the gear shift and the scent of vinegar on your breath when you kissed me from across the car. I'd do anything to be back there, anything at all. But you are gone, and I am here in London Fields and the sun is shining and another leaf falls from a tree, like shedding skin, and I'm okay without you, I am. And maybe on my way home to bake bread I'll stop by the butchery and if they have a nice chicken with good yellow fat, I'll buy one for broth. And I'll remember to ask them to pluck those last few feathers from the wings, don't worry. It's getting chilly now and my fingers are cracking at the knuckles and stiff as a board.

Forever missing you, Marcus

London Independent Story Prize 1st Round Finalist

Tracy Fahey

THE WOMEN IN THE WATER

The first time I hear about Scéine, we're moving house. To Waterville. I trace the Irish name for the village on the map. *Inbhear Scéine.*

'Scéine's harbour.' I'm proud of my Irish. 'Who was Scéine?'

My mother half-turns in the van, smiles. 'She's part of an old story told round these parts.'

The miles tick by. She tells me of the Milesians who sailed to Ireland, bent on revenging themselves on the Tuatha de Danann who had killed their king. It was a difficult voyage, she says. The de Danann sent druidic winds into the harbour to overturn their ships.

My father hums under his breath, soft, then louder

'And Scéine drowned in the harbour. But her husband Amergin took her to shore and buried her where the stone circle stands today.'

I pick at the frayed seat back. 'But who was she?'

My father's back tenses. 'For God's sake, it's only a story.'

'She was Amerigan's wife,' says my mother.

#

I find a thin piece of pale green sea-glass, in the rough shape of a woman. I touch it. Scéine. Not in her grave, but anchored deep in the water of the harbour. Her limbs twined with seaweed, fish flickering around her. She stands on one

37

foot, one arm pointing to the surface. Her tiara crusted with barnacles.

I ask about her, but no-one knows more. She is a whisper, a breath on the wind.

My father drills a hole in the glass. I wear it round my neck on a bootlace.

#

I find the sea-glass in an old jacket pocket when I unpack at Falmouth. I drop my blue swimsuit on the bed. From the window the sea glistens silver, strip-lit by a pale sun. I pull the frayed bootlace over my head, running a thumb over the slight grain of the glass.

I look up Sceine in a book of early Irish history. One footnote. She was a female satirist. A poet. Like me.

#

I love it here. The Cornish folk songs in the pub sound like home, but my tiny flat is quiet. Instead of voices arguing, the distant hiss of waves. I sit in the library and read through stacks of books, some of them on my Literature course, most not. The pile of poems in the drawer grows; black ink scrawl on cream paper.

And the sea. Warmer than I'm used to, the path down to it a nest of palms, silhouetted against a blue sky. There's a rock out in the bay. I dream of reaching it.

So I swim out every day, each day a little further.

#

Maybe today is the day.

I'm three-quarters of the way out to the rock when I feel it. A cramp slashes my side. I stop, tread water, panting. To the rock or back? Icy muscles of undercurrent push against me.

Back.

I strike out. The cramp rips across my stomach, I double up, splutter a stream of bubbles. Something brushes my ankle, slides eel-like across it. The cramp is a knife now. I try to tread water again, but I'm sinking, fast.

I'm under, eyes open, panicked. Through the gloom a flash of white stretches up.

A hand.

#

Choking, retching, spitting. My face plastered in wet sand.

He stands over me; big, tanned, his blue eyes anxious. 'You OK?'

The sea-glass pendant is twisted round my throat. I pull it off, wipe my face. A group of surfers clustered behind him. One girl puts a hand on his arm. He shakes her off. 'Stop, Sal.'

Drops glitter on his face. He smiles, takes my hand. 'Matt.'

He closes his hand so tight round mine, the sea-glass cracks in two. Blood drips through my fingers.

#

I wish that was the only time Matt hurt me. But it's not.

He's lovely at first. And so handsome I catch my breath. My tiny flat fills with him. His surfboard leaves a black mark on my wall.

The girl called Sal watches me with him. One day she tries to talk to me.

'Come on.' Matt pulls me away from her. That night when I hand him a plate of paella, he deliberately lets it smash on the stone flags.

His moods rise like sea-storms; abrupt, unexpected. After a while I stop trying to guess. I stop a lot of things he doesn't like.

Writing.

Swimming.

'What if you get in trouble?' he says.

Too late.

#

I drop out of university. We move inland. Somewhere no-one knows us, cares enough to ask about my bruises. Instead of the crash of waves, the snarl of traffic. I keep my memories in a box, like my drift of poems, the broken sea-glass.

My mother is ill. Matt doesn't want to but he finally lets me go. I pack a few things. By the time I get there, she's lost consciousness, submerged in dreams. Her eyes roll under wrinkled lids. From the open window, the fresh tang of seaweed.

In the kitchen, the sound of my father banging doors, rattling pans. I hold my mother's cold hand tight in mine.

She revives once that night. Smiles at me, that slow, warm smile. 'You need to go for a swim.'

It's the last thing she will say. Dreaming, she goes out with the tide.

#

I go down to the strand. Around my throat, the old sea-glass amulet, glued together.

Surfers dot the sea, heads bob up and down, seal-shiny. I pull off my dress. Underneath, my old blue swimsuit.

I wade out to mid-thigh. A cold wind sleets across the surface. In the darkness around my legs, a flash of white limbs. *Scéine*. Beside her, more women. Delicate and translucent as jellyfish. Their bodies poems written in water.

I tremble. But their arms reach out, hold me steady. Around me, a chorus of sound rises like smoke.

You have a voice.

I breast the waves; they're icy, glorious.

London Independent Story Prize 1st Round Finalist

Rosie Parry

What You Can Expect

> 1. **Withdrawal from the External World**. As the end-of-life approaches, there is a feeling of detachment from the physical world and a loss of interest in things formerly found pleasurable.

When the lift starts up again Carole pretends to be relieved. She wants out. Away from the stinging antiseptic smell, away from the tinny voice of her captor. But then again, she doesn't really want to arrive at her mother's bedroom either.

Perhaps the only solution is the one that's just presented itself: to stay here, suspended somewhere between coming and going forever. Immobile but incapable of doing anything about it, the whole thing totally out of her hands now.

Failing that, she'd like to go down to the hospital canteen and inhale a potato dog.

Do you know what that is? Imagine a sausage roll but encased in deep fried batter instead of pastry. Seems like the kind of thing that should be illegal in a hospital, but what can you do? The nurses might roll their eyes, sure, but they're too busy taking blood and cleaning chest ports to start lobbying the canteen for healthier snacks. Besides, there'll be all kinds of regulations for the suppliers and whatnot. Politics. Anyway, Carole has been eating about three a week since her mother was admitted.

The lift groans. Shudders. Stops again. Jesus fuck.

Excuse me? The voice comes through the help panel. Did you say something?

Yes, sorry. Carole leans in. Sorry, I was just saying it's stopped again.

Okay love. Don't worry. We'll get you out.

-

Dark already by the time she gets home.

Her phone is nearly dead. She sits down heavily, sagging into the sofa cushions. She registers the spread of her thighs, the pinch at her waistband. If she wants dinner she'll have to get going, the supermarket is closing soon. She needs toilet paper too, and – even making the list exhausts her.

She doesn't mean to sleep but as soon as her eyes close, just to rest, just to rest, she's out. Dreaming of grinding metal gears and needles and then suddenly He's calling. Lately she's been trying to let it ring for a bit before she answers, but tonight she can't help herself.

> 2. **Breathlessness.** Some people feel breathless or short of breath. You might hear this called dyspnoea. It can be made worse if the person is anxious. The doctor or nurse may give medicine for breathlessness or advise practical steps, like having a fan in the room or opening a window.

Carole isn't sheltered. She's seen enough internet porn to know that other women do it with their hands, or sometimes with a toy. But Carole can only manage on her front, a pillow clamped tight between her thighs. After she hangs up, she can't bring herself to move from the sofa to the bedroom, because this means squeezing down the hallway, past the mirrors her mother hung to give the impression that their little home was full of space, and light. Instead, she sleeps where she is, trousers nestled in the crook of her arm, head resting on the scratchy fabric.

3. **Changing toilet habits.** Because a dying person is eating and drinking less, their bowel movements may reduce. They may pass less solid waste less often. They may also urinate less frequently.

The next day her favourite Doctor is there. Carole can never remember his last name. Something like Dunn or Duncan maybe? But she loves Doctor Whatshisface for his soft features and how he slowly explains things to her mother, even though he knows she can no longer understand.

I'm taking your hand now, Jane. I'm going to have the nurse come in and take your blood, Jane. Jane, I'm afraid there's not much good news.

This is mainly why he visits, to tell them something bad. Today that is: Jane's liver is failing and soon she will die.

How soon we can't say.

But you have some idea? Not an exact day then, but a window? A week? Surely not less than a week?

After he leaves, she spends a long time staring at the mottled purple bruise that's spread around the catheter in her mother's hand. She doesn't hear the nurse come in, or the first two times she says hello. The third time she gently places a hand on Carole's arm. This nurse is especially good at these bits, the shoulder squeezing and nice-face-making. They're all so good here, angels, really. Carole knows this is what you're supposed to say. But when she thinks about angels, she thinks about Dr Who and the Orthodox hymns her friend Anastasia shared with her, in which angels are awesome and frightening. The nurses are the same. They know all of the things we try not to remember, too much about the body and how it can break. All the weaknesses you must forget in order to get out of bed, get dressed and venture out into the world of sharp objects and speeding cars.

The nurse keeps reassuring Carole that they'll call if anything happens. The purple is spreading, seeping across her mother's parchment skin. She says Carole must look after herself too, must get some rest. The skin is so thin Carole can hardly believe it keeps everything inside. It's not until the nurse asks if there's anyone who could come and pick Carole up that she realises what is happening and gathers her things to leave.

She avoids the lift, taking the stairs instead. But of course, these stairs are only meant for the staff and the door on the ground floor won't open without a fob. She clambers back up to the ward, her thighs burning, but it's the same problem. She is, once again, trapped in the in-between. Except this time her knees are aching, and her mother is nearly dead. She worries that if she starts hammering on the door she won't be able to stop. Who could she phone? Who could possibly be waiting for her at either end? Exhausted again, she leans her head on the door.

44

Thunk.

A nurse is staring at her, his eyes wide. Sorry, he mouths. Carole stands aside and he lets her back into the ward. The stairs are only for the nurses.

Yes, sorry. Sorry, I know.

-

It seems strange to Carole that the visitor canteen stays open after visiting hours. Probably seemed strange to the boy behind the till that a smartly dressed woman came and bought a heft of deep-fried snacks right before closing too, but neither of them said anything. She eats them in the car, one after the other, until her stomach pulses and she gags, flecks of batter smattering the dashboard.

4. **Experiencing confusion.** When a person is dying, their brain is still very active. However, they may become confused or incoherent at times. This may happen if they lose track of what is happening around them.

We've started near the end, but we could have picked up anywhere in the last six months and it would have been much the same. Carole wakes up. She dresses quickly, sometimes without showering, always without much thought as to the combined effect of her clothes. Then she goes about her day, which used to mean more than going to the hospital and maybe to the shop. Mostly, she waits. For the phone to ring. For news from the hospital. On a good night He calls. Sometimes, when she is feeling especially brave, they talk a little. With the right prompting she can sometimes bring herself to move her mouth around all those hard C sounds. *Co..ck...cun..t..come...* Comes quite naturally after a while, even for Carole, who didn't have a boyfriend until she was nearly thirty.

5. **Talking less,** (or if they're a child, more).

She is not in the right mood for drinking, but suddenly here she is, drinking warm wine in her neighbour's kitchen.

As soon as he spots her Michael is careering over. Carole! Welcome! Her face feels painfully dry and tight. Michael has always liked her, ever since he moved in. This is much to the frustration of beautiful Jenny, her other neighbour, who is, for some reason, married to Michael.

Carole has never liked Michael but sometimes it's nice to feel a little special so she lets him talk her into a stupor in the corner, him getting drunker and louder, Carole feeling herself get smaller and smaller and smaller until he's asking about her mother and she's saying we had a bit of bad news actually and then there really is no stopping him.

Carole... He's saying, his breath wet on her neck. It does get better... This is the worst part... Oh and when it's over of course it's hard... But this is the worst bit, definitely... Hanging around death all day... Well, it's no fun for anyone... No look, I'm just saying... No listen... I'm not upsetting her... Am I... Am I... Carole, I'm not upsetting you... All I'm saying... All I'm saying is you need to get through this and then get out there again... Get yourself a friend... boyfriend... maybe... We must make room for the living! God knows, you're an attractive lady Carole...

46

The air around them is growing increasingly still, chatter from the other guests petering out as they strain to hear what Michael is saying, could possibly be saying, to have provoked such a public display of emotion from the normally quiet Carole. All around the room the other guests are making eyes at each other, appalled, amused, mostly just desperate to look at anything but Jenny's stoney face, and Carole, who is properly sobbing now.

6. **Increasing pain.** It can be difficult to come to terms with the unavoidable fact that a person's pain levels may increase as they near death.

Michael, Jenny says, you are needed in the garden.

Alone again, Carole heads to the bathroom. There, she takes in the cursive labels declaring *SOAP* or *TOWELS*, in the same font that on the other side of the door exclaims *LOO*. She scrolls through her phone, her finger hovering over His number. But he's never been interested in anything other than late night panting. When this is over, she will find someone else, a proper boyfriend.

Carole stares into the toilet bowl. Maybe it's like tea leaves. Despite herself, she laughs. She already knows that a future is impossible. Her life is cleaved into two distinct parts, the first forty-something years and then this second part. The part in which she has felt a human hand grow weak and waxy in her own and seen a tube filled with flecks of her mother's blood.

She heads back to the kitchen to get a drink and finds Susie sitting on the counter. Sorry, Susie says, dad's a moron. Susie is burning little pieces of plastic with a lighter and swinging her legs, leaving black smudges where her shoes have collided with the white cabinet. Any other time Carole might have told her off for this, she has the same cabinets in her kitchen next door and knows how they stain. But fuck Micheal and fuck his cabinets.

Michael reappears, looking very tired. Anyone for another glass of this? He brandishes a bottle of something expensive looking, eyes fixed firmly on the floor.

7. **Active dying is the final phase of the dying process.** While the pre-active stage lasts for about three weeks, the active stage of dying lasts roughly three days.

We must make room for the living. God. Carole lies in bed and worries about the weeds in her garden. She's drunk still. She notices a crack in the ceiling. Her feet are sweating. She thinks, I must wash my hair before I leave the house tomorrow. She thinks, it would be so satisfying to cut Michael's hands off with a bread knife. She thinks about what the nice Doctor's mouth tastes like and then thinks he's probably too young to think about. Her eyes are stinging, nearly there now. Mum. No, not now Carole. The phone is ringing.

8. **Moment of death.** It's not always clear when the exact moment of death occurs. When a person dies, those around them may notice that their face suddenly relaxes and looks peaceful. If the death isn't completely peaceful, it's unlikely that the person will have been aware of it.

48

It's quiet on the ward tonight. The nice Doctor, whose name is actually nothing like Duncan or Dunn, but Taylor, is watching over Jane. Well, half watching, half thinking about how his girlfriend asked him to hit her in the face while they were at it last night. He refused, but he's missing her now. Maybe he should have given it a go, at least.

He is always touched by the little trinkets the families bring in. Framed photos are especially good, he thinks, because they remind everyone who enters the room to check a drip or change a bedpan that the person in the bed had a whole life before they arrived on the ward. A life filled with hot air balloon festivals and fat, flaxen babies and nearly always a dog. It disturbs him when the wedding photos are high quality, in full colour. Surely, they should be black and white, ancient. Jane's daughter brings her mother flowers every week, daffodils and daisies. It all adds up to something, doesn't it?

Carole's mother isn't thinking anything at all. It's not so bad, here in Painkiller Land. Icy water and something frying somewhere. Big, black sheets of linen. A warm snow. Just a mouth and a couple of lungs and a couple of eyes that can no longer see and a couple more breaths and ah, there we go.

London Independent Story Prize 2nd Round Finalist

Samuel Prince

CHANCE IS A RESTLESS TRAVELLER

Even when they realised the tube was shut, they stood in front of the padlocked gates and waited. Word spread this may be terminal. Still, they waited. Others joined the scrum sharing the news which came in drips and fractured clips. The station was closed, the line was down, the entire Underground network suspended. The overall picture emerged, then misted to speculation. No-one could establish the cause. It was a temporary fault, then localised protest, then industrial strike. The official verdict was a catastrophic power loss due to unforeseen events. As this filtered through, the crowd outside Mornington Crescent began to disband. Hissing buses pulled up to crammed stops. Passengers on-board glared spleen at those alighting.

Reece set-off down Eversholt Street. Everything supercharged from docile to delirious - the fresh gauze of morning stripped off - as the traffic snarled and the streets began to prosper with people. Kings Cross pulsed with commotion. Buses backed-up. Shouts, horns, squalls of exhaust. Walkers consulted their phone screens. The official verdict was sticking for now. Reece turned onto a Gray's Inn Road choked with cars. She raised her Pentax and snapped a junction impasse. There was shade, sheen, aggression and blossom – her first picture of the day.

She didn't need music. The tube disturbance seemed to equalise everyone to the same frequency. Hyper-alert, infused with the crowds, purposeful, but running late. She thought about the sequence of her thoughts, their lack of connective tissue. She berated herself for the things that came to mind. Thoughts weren't evidence for anything. They were swerves and stunts, isolated phenomena. She knew who she was. She was the reflection prowling past tall windows at ground level. She shoulder-rolled to evade the surge. She was the conserver of her body. She didn't jaywalk or risk it in her fawn espadrilles. She had a canvas rucksack and carried the camera on a neck-strap. She wasn't arbiter for the atomic tap-tap in her head.

*

He'd never been there before. Outside Farringdon Station, in the heart of the commuter cross-fire. Sat at a blue cloth-covered picnic table in dark faux-Edwardian get-up. He wore a top hat and cape. The three cup and ball game - £3 to play. Keep your eye on the cup containing the ball and the correct call doubles your money. The rules were displayed simply on a desk placard. People marched past and gave no notice. People glanced back. People frowned and turned heel. Stragglers at the station gates stared. Nobody paid, nobody played. Reece circled the table at a distance. It was a gift shot she couldn't find the angle for. Too much dawdling and human blur.

Cleaners in the communal kitchen. Plates, slams. The dishwasher gawping. The kettle berserks to boiling. A weeping phone goes unconsoled. Monitors slur, printers bicker. Folders, files, synthetic plants. Here they come. Greetings, grunts. The tube outage is a failsafe to build the unpleasantries around. The disruption, the delay, the disorder. Some send dispatches and estimated arrivals mid-journey. Convoluted routes are recounted like tawdry odysseys.

The cooler slobbers. Reece sinks a piercing draught. She skins a clementine with her index nail. A colleague, Tess, slid a saucer-shaped rice cake in her mouth while mumbling about the tube.

"It was a nightmare. I waited for three buses, before I decided to walk."
"I walk, anyway", Reece replied.
"It just makes you think, when that happens. When no-one knows what's going on."
Reece looked up as Tess continued: "We just don't know, do we? We only know what we're told. It makes you think..."
"Or overthink."

Tess dialled a dab of cream cheese around her plate. 'I've started paying attention to exits. In a restaurant, if I'm sitting, I want to face the door. It used to be I wanted full sight of the room or the window, but now, it's the door'.

Reece nodded to quietly signal the end of her interest, although she thought through her options for defence in that scenario: cutlery, plates, glasses, bottles, chairs. She flipped the lid of her laptop and woke it up. She couldn't see what nobody knew was coming.

*

They sat clustered around the rectangular table. Marker pens, like spent cartridges, were scattered across it. Bret stood pointing at the flat screen with a biro. The team's names were tiered in a column on the left-hand side. On

52

horizontal axis were the week commencing dates for the next three months. The board was a mosaic of ticks, question marks and crosses, to denote availability and capacity. Reece's name was seventh down. She confirmed she was mostly ticks. She doodled three x's in her notebook.

There was frenzy below. They all craned to look down through the window. People were evacuating the building opposite. Fire marshals in luminous gilets were leading them down the street. It was unhurried, procedural. The verge of a shambles.

"Just a drill," someone said.
"False alarm," someone replied.
"Makes you think," another reasoned.

Bret told them to move away from the windows and lowered the blinds with a remote control.

"Just in case," he explained.

*

Reece watched a man raking mown grass in the churchyard. She sat on a bench beneath the spire of St James's Church. Savannah had called and she came here to talk.

"You were saying last week, you were beginning to feel differently?"
"The exercises helped," Reece said. "The more I wrote down, in the sequence you suggested, the easier it became to spot the patterns."
"Good, good. Keep that up. You don't need to always use the paper grids - you can adapt it how you please." She paused. "And what about the other things we discussed?"

Reece had sat with Savannah in the clinic on the Caledonian Road for four sessions now. Savannah placed both palms on her stomach while she listened. She took no notes, referred to no papers. On her last visit, as she talked, Reece gazed at the chair by Savannah's side. A coat hung from the back and a Tupperware box sat on the cushion. Reece could see it was congested with salad leaves, lettuce and cucumber. She imagined it riven with beetles – Savannah unwittingly forking all acrawl things into her mouth in a hasty lunch hour.

"I still struggle with denial. I struggle with sabotage. I can't accept I can make the choices I want." The groundsman wore a navy boiler suit with the Council insignia on the back. He shook out a refuse bag and tied a knot with two ends.

Savannah sounded soother, but more cautious. "I understand. And we'll work on that. In the meantime, you have to remember the technique of erasing yourself from the picture. Think how the situation would look if your mind wasn't involved."

Reece computed this slowly. "It makes you think," she defaulted. She stood up from the bench. Her head felt unmoored.

*

He'd attracted a curious crowd. The ferreting lunch-seekers of early afternoon bypassed him, but as Reece walked back to the office she stopped again to look. A gang of boys wearing identical orange backpacks were humming around his table. One of the boys was haggling to play. Reece clocked them for tourists. The boy warily offered a note and the thimblerigger gestured grandly with his hat. He was opulently bald. He held the small ball for the crowd to see then snuck it in the middle cup and turned all three over.

His fingers flexed. The game commenced. He moved the inverted tumblers slowly, labouredly, at first. The rotations were pronounced and easy to follow. The boys pointed and filmed him with their mobiles. One of their crew went behind the table to follow the action from the thimblerigger's perspective. The movement quickened, the tumblers scraped. His hands seemed to merge as he spun the cups like a demonic mixmaster. The boys jostled, they lost the pace. Reece trained her camera, waited, but didn't shoot. A larger crowd had begun to mill around the scene. Shirts, cuffs, pinstripe - sharp cut attire. More phones, videos, rubbernecking at the fuss. Then cries of awe, mock lament. The thimblerigger won. The orange backpacks thawed. The crowd tapered to the still curious. She fixed the lens cap. No one was moving him on.

*

The leaving card was waiting on her desk. On the front, it said *Good Luck in the New Job* in a garish script. Someone had snuck a list of names inside. Reece crossed hers out and contemplated the other messages. They were virtually identical. Everybody had scrawled the same banality or bromide. It looked like a petition. She didn't know Mark well – who the card was for. He worked on the legal team. Reece sometimes saw him in the morning panting up the stairs carrying his road bike. He wore green Lycra shorts, a breathable jersey and sports sunglasses. She'd never talked to him. Her pen dithered. She thought about the tube situation, the dormancy of Farringdon station at lunch. *Today is a good day to be you*, she wrote, and signed-off.

Tess took the card. Reece checked the news. All lines were still down. The cause still unknown. Pictures of men in hi-vis vests around station entrances. Videos of commuters roaming confused. Live updates told nothing.

She thought about the conversation with Savannah. She mulled over *evidence for the thought* and her head stalled. She whispered the word "choice" to herself. She made the cursor on her screen spiral.

"Choice." She began to type because she had to.

*

Getting home owned the room. The office had gathered in a breakout zone for a farewell to Mark. Speeches, cheers. Cake, fizz. Napkins, crumbs. Everyone had a plan. Buses, bikes, taxi share, pub, bar – decide later. A wall mounted TV told of tentative solutions. Full power restored by the morning. Someone proposed a lock-in at the office. Guffaws, groans.

Tess handed Reece a flute of bubbles. Mark opened a leaving gift – a cycling shirt with the company logo on the reverse. Contagious laughter and whoops. Mark posed for photos. Reece retreated to her desk. She tipped the flute's contents into a plastic Yucca pot, took her bag and headed discretely for the stairs.

The city purred in early evening haze. Scabs of moss and lichen defaced the flat-roof. She'd climbed the stairwell up here. She'd propped the fire door with an extinguisher so she could walk out, get away and survey. She looked out across the buildings. The metro-muteness. The cloud smears and contrails. The cranes and aerials. The day losing its nerve and tang. Reece thought of the thousands down there, headless to get home. Those consulting maps, timetables, distances, as the crow flies and contingencies. She thought of Savannah's lunch box. She pictured it empty, devoured of leaves. An unwashed fork in the avocado grease.

A day fringed with mystery. A day of suspense and stasis. When she said "Choice," she felt her inner cheeks strive to meet. When she said "chance," her chest sighed, deflated.

*

By the time she descended, the office was all dregs and party dereliction. A cleaner was spooling streamers into a bin bag. Reece watched her through a glass partition. She could see the TV news still fixated on the tube. A reporter was stood on a bridge gesturing at the walking throng.

Night was curdling, cooling. Farringdon station was still chained shut. Emergency tape was slathered across the gates. A somewhere woman yelled "Where are you going," from Cowcross Street and Reece felt a sudden chill. The thimblerigger hadn't budged. He was unoccupied, but motionless. He smiled as she approached.

She paid up front and placed the ball under the middle tumbler. She stepped back from the table. He nodded. "Do it," she said. He fluttered his fingers. She was her choices. She wasn't her thoughts. There wasn't a chance. He whisked the cups with ostentation. She took out her camera. She clicked. His hands fast-danced.

London Independent Story Prize 2nd Round Finalist

Georgia Boon

The Wound on Francesca Miller's Arm

The worst thing about Mum's heart attack was that it happened right outside my school. If you include the sixth form, that's maybe two thousand students looking at my Mum's cold-custard arse in those bright blue running leggings that stop everyone else's thighs from wobbling, but can't seem to stop hers. Two thousand witnesses to my Mum's blotchy running face looking even blotchier than usual. If there was a pie chart showing the proportion of the students who knew that it was *my* Mum who had fallen in the Swindon coach layby, then that pie chart would be a single colour. *Everyone* knew.

Ms Gannicox, the school secretary, who always walks on tiptoes and has a voice like a therapy app, came to get me out of class. Ms Tapscott the physics teacher, flicked her hair and pouted like she always does when someone interrupts her Brian Cox impersonation: acting out the expansion of space, or a bike pulling another stupid bike along by a piece of elastic.

'Right, Cerys,' Gannicox said, all breathy, and I could tell by her tone that there would be no chance of a vape between here and wherever she was taking me. 'It's your Mum. She's here.'

My stomach did the thing it does when Mum comes in my room without knocking, even if I'm only watching Call the Midwife; or when she texts to ask why my location isn't on when I'm supposed to be at Lara's, but we're in the woods.

'What does she want?'

The secretary stopped and listened for a moment. A siren, a few streets away.

'Sorry, I've said it wrong, haven't I? I mean she's outside the school. She's ill. An ambulance is on its way, Cerys.'

'Outside *this* school?' I said, pressing my lips together and shaking my head. It's what I do when someone says something out of order. 'Shut up!' This didn't even draw a blink from Gannicox.

Outside, the ambulance had turned a corner onto the road and was tootling along with its lights flashing and its little tune playing. It reversed to come level with the pavement, crunching over bits of broken bike light and an old puff-bar case. I stopped myself thinking about how thick its tyres must be. That could have taken me dangerously close to voluntarily answering a physics question.

I tried looking down at Mum. She was holding her shoulder, her eyes squeezed shut. The skin on her face underneath the blotches was a sort of dull colour, like my white Brandy Melville t-shirt after she put it in the wash with that stupid navy tea towel. There were kids behind the fence, summoned by the sirens, and Mr McGowan patrolling up and down and telling them not to look, to go back inside, but while his legs were doing this silly little march, his eyes were on her, on my Mum. Mum made a sort of breathing sound and I thought 'I hate you,' which was also the last thing I'd said to her before I'd left that morning.

The ambulance started rattling open its doors. I didn't expect them to be so loud, to make the same sound as the Sainsbury's van. It was a Tuesday and that was the night they usually came. Me and Mum always argued when the shopping arrived. She kept ordering things I liked to eat when I was seven. Petits Filous? Jesus.

'You used to like them,' she said last week.

'*Used to* being the important part of that sentence.'

'You need more calcium. Those little bones are growing, you know.'

The inside of the ambulance looked nothing like a Sainsbury's van. It looked like a slice of hospital. I've only been in a hospital once. Mum let me visit Granny before she got too ill. She had a red lump on her calf. It was on display, her leg sticking out from under the sheet. I whispered to Mum to ask her to cover it up but she said shush first and then, no, that it would hurt too much. I didn't believe her. Mum spent all her time there, days and days, and I had to go to Mrs Glender's and drink powdery squash from plastic cups with rough bits round the rim.

The ambulance person told us all to move back. He had a man bun. In my opinion, all emergency services workers should have a plain bowl cut of Lego hair. You don't want to have to think about *who* this person is. You want them to

60

be a machine. To embody the role, like Ms Carter says we should in drama.

Another ambulance person appeared, an elaborate plait knocking into their back, and they were holding the paddles, and the one with the man bun sort of unfolded Mum and was saying things, her name, and what they're going to do, and that they're going to pull her top up and loosen her bra and I was gone. I hate you, I thought, extra loud, all the way back up the field, everyone looking at me, all the sixth formers there, and the popular group from the year above, and I thought maybe *my* heart would pop, explode in my chest, and they'd get to see *my* disgusting fucking bra as well as my Mum's, because she would only buy my the plain t-shirt ones from M&S and not a balcony one from Victoria's Secret which is literally what everyone else has. Even Lara.

Soon Gannicox was running up the field behind me, those little steps. I pretended not to notice and easily made it inside in time to shut the door in her face.

'Cerys, did you not want to go with your Mum?' she said, panting once she reached me in the corridor. When I didn't say anything, she said, 'I expect it wouldn't have been nice, watching those shocks going through her.' I hadn't thought about that, the paddles being anything other than props from a TV show.

'I've got Chemistry after break, Miss. Don't want to miss my chance to be a woman in STEM.'

'Well, if you're sure. They've said she'll be fine. Or should be fine.' She squeezed her face up into a smile.

Chemistry was alright because of the new seating plan they put in after Oscar loosened the screws in Allegra's chair and she'd ended up splayed across the front of the class.

At lunch, old Gannicox was back again, asking if I wanted to phone the hospital? Or if there was anyone else I wanted to call? That was the first time that day I'd thought about my Dad. As well as being too stupid not to have a heart attack outside my school, my Mum is too stupid to leave my Dad. How anyone can share their life with someone so utterly devoid of content I will never know. But there she is, having dinner with him every night. *Making conversation.* That's what they call it when one person has to do all the work: literally *make* conversation.

When I got home from school, Dad wanted to know why I hadn't called him. Did I think that adults had some kind of communication system like sonar? Mum had been in the hospital for an hour, he said, before they called him. He could have been there with her that whole time, holding her hand, comforting her. I made a throw-up sound, and for the first time ever, Dad stormed out of the room on *me.*

When Dad he walked into my room later, no knocking, he said Mum wouldn't be coming home that night. They were keeping her in. There was a clattering outside. The Sainsbury's van.

*

Everyone was all head dipped and eyes lowered at school the next day. No-one said anything, but they were all acting how they did around Tyler after his Dad did himself in. Dad said in the morning that he was going to see Mum that afternoon. But maybe it would be best if I came once she was a bit a better? He put an orange Club bar in my bag.

'There, I know you like them,' he said.

Later, when I got home, he was already back. He seemed to have given up going to work.

'Good news!' he said, springing up from the sofa and trying to take my hand. 'She should be discharged tomorrow. They've put a stent into her artery. Here, I got this leaflet that explains it.' I took it from him. 'It's ok if you don't feel like talking. I'll leave it there.'

*

In my room, I took the Club biscuit out of my bag. There's no way I could have eaten it at school. It's a proper chav snack. I nibbled the chocolate from round the edges while I read the leaflet. Nothing better to do in this cultural dessert. There were pictures of how they put the little bit of chicken wire in your vein to prop it up. I tried to imagine one in my heart. Or lots of little bits of chicken wire, in a ring, making the valves open and close in time, keeping me alive for ever, like an immortal cyborg. But when I tried to think of a stent in Mum's heart, I couldn't see it, couldn't picture her heart. When I tried to think about what was beneath her breastbone, there was just nothing.

*

Francesca Miller is the girl who can quote whole chunks of Shakespeare in an essay and do standard deviation without a calculator. But she does not have a single friend. Her Mum still walks her into school, and hands over a bag of Dairylea sandwiches with the crusts cut off before kissing her goodbye. Her Mum has this kind of haircut that's for an old person who sits under one of those heaters they don't have any more in hairdresser's. Francesca doesn't care. She doesn't care that no-one speaks to her; that she's picked first in PE so that the team captain can get it over with before they get told off by the teacher for leaving it too late. That once, Digby Thatcher made a collage of photos of her face where she looked like she was taking a dump and used it as the background to a biology Powerpoint on the digestive system.

I've always sat next to Francesca in History. She stopped talking to me in year eight when I told her in the middle of her explaining to me where the stones at Stonehenge had come from, that if I ever heard her voice again I would put glue in her hair and mould it into the shape of a turd on the top of her head. But on the Friday after Mum's heart attack, she spoke to me again.

Mum still hadn't come home. The stent was taking longer to work than it should have done. Plus the cut from where she had fallen was infected. Apparently she had torn up the front of one leg when she fell, all across the knee. I hadn't noticed. And now everyone was saying it was cellulitis, like I knew what that was. Dad brought a leaflet home about that as well. It had pictures of cross-sections of cells with little trails of worms writhing through them. That was the cellulitis, apparently. While I was looking at the leaflet, Dad held the phone out to me with Mum was on loud speaker, and he told me to say something. I'd pressed my lips together and shook my head. When I was falling asleep that night, I closed my eyes and saw those little worms squirming around in Mum's chest, right where her heart should have been.

'How's your Mum doing?' Francesca said and I lifted up the copy of the GCSE textbook, 'Britain, Health and the People c.1000 - Present Day' and brought it down on her arm and then looked with surprise at what I had been able to achieve. There was a deep gash and I gasped and sprang back and when I shut my eyes, I could see diagrams of the cells splitting apart like in the leaflet.

Ms Gannicox wasn't on reception that day, so Creepy Creece came to collect me from the corridor to take me to Townsend, the Head. Creece is the PE teacher with a double chin and skinny legs that make her look like a picture in one of those games where you draw a little bit of an imaginary person and then fold up the paper and pass it to the next person so they can't see what you've done. She gripped my wrist so hard that she may as well have been giving me a Chinese burn. My other hand was covered in blood and I kept thinking she would take me to wash it off before she took me to Mr Townsend. But that didn't happen and so while I stood outside his office after I'd knocked, staring at the laminated picture of 'The Wheel of Success' blu-tacked on the door, the blood was drying and getting cold and making it feel sort of like cramp.

Mr Townsend's room smelled different to any other part of the school, something similar to the airing cupboard at home.

Creepy Creece was saying that Mr Townsend had asked me a question.

He repeated himself, asking what punishment I thought I deserved.

I tried to swallow but the back of my throat felt thick. I looked down, riveted by the carpet.

Creece was saying something about it not having been an easy couple of weeks, and Mr Townsend was nodding and muttering something about Mum.

The carpet tiles were made up of four different colours which I hadn't ever noticed before. Altogether they just made blue.

I tried saying something but my mouth was as dry as when the dentist sucks all the spit out with the sucker before they start tapping along your teeth with that poky metal thing.

Creepy Creece asked me to give them a minute and there I was back at the Wheel of Success. I expected Creece was telling Townsend about the time I'd not been able to stop laughing when she kept saying 'karate' with a weird Japanese accent; or the time I'd tricked Amber Sullivan into carrying a bag of shotputs that Creece had told me I had to personally take to the games shed ('Here, Amber, feel how heavy these are.' Works every time).

I got it into my head that when I went back in, they would say that they were going to drive me to the hospital and when they did, a nurse would take me over to Francesa and lift her bandage and make me look at the wound and then my Mum would appear and she would look at the wound as well and then she'd say the bandage had to be left off in case it was hurting Francesca's arm and now I could see it, picture it very clearly, the blood driving through Mum's chest, her pipes, all the tiny bits of chicken wire, and into her heart. And she looked up at me and shook her head, ashamed.

But that wasn't what they said at all. Townsend said that Creece had explained a little more to him about the situation with Mum, and what a difficult time it must be. There would be consequences, of course, but most likely suspension for a few days.

I wiped my face and shrugged.

*

Dad made me play Cluedo with him for four nights in a row, even though I explained you weren't supposed to play it with two people. He didn't seem to care, just kept rolling the dice, and saying, 'I am able to assist you with your enquiries,' and then showing me whatever card I'd asked about, but as though there were loads of people in the room, showing it really secretly, not like it was just me and him.

I won every time and then he went on the phone to Mum for a while while I got ready for bed.

Dad said that when Mum came home, she might need to have some special equipment with her. But not to let that worry me. He hadn't told her about the suspension, or about Francesca Miller. Not the right time he said, in a sort of whisper.

The night after I was allowed to go back to school, we cleaned the house together. Mum would be home the next day. Dad folded up a blanket on her pillow.

'There, she'll like that,' he said. But I knew it was the itchy one that she didn't like so I got the one off my bed and Dad folded it and put it on the pillow instead.

At nine, while I was brushing my teeth, I heard the Sainsbury's van doors rattle outside the window.

She'd put the order in from her phone and texted Dad to say there were some extra treats for me.

We unpacked it together. There were cheese strings and fruit winders and some bottles of apple and blackcurrant with twisty lids. I felt all slow while I was putting things in the cupboards.

Dad asked me how school had been. If anyone had said anything. I didn't tell him that no one spoke to me the entire day; that I gave the whole place my deadest eyes, my chin in the air.

The bandage on Francesca's arm was quite small, more of a dressing, really. They'd done a new seating plan that put us on opposite sides of the room, but I couldn't stop looking across. I wanted to see the wound, to get it over with. It would be so odd to ask her. 'Can you lift it up, please? Your dressing? I want to see your wound while it's fresh, before it turns into a scar.' Almost as odd as when Calvin asked to see underneath Kelsey's tongue in year seven. Weirdo.

But I did think that when Mum got home, I might ask her. If I could see under her bandages. If I could place my hand, right there, and feel it, her heart, and the chicken wire, and the whole thing, pumping away, and maybe she would look at me and I would be able to find something to say to her.

I didn't answer Dad's questions about how school had been. Taking questions about school days is against policy. You start giving them information like that and it never stops. Next thing they'll be telling you how *they* feel and there's no coming back from that.

Suddenly I remembered something. I don't know why the stupid thought came to me then. But it was something Dad had asked me the night before. What had I said to her, he wanted to know, while she was lying there. I must have said something?

'It's just,' Dad had said, 'I'll bet she was pleased to see you. That whatever you said comforted her.'

I didn't tell him I hadn't said anything. What's going to make you feel better when your literal heart has literally stopped? Again, I tried to picture that happening, the tubes, the pipes, but I couldn't see it.

London Independent Story Prize 2nd Round Finalist

Patrick Cash

The Dragon

I once believed I could save a man. We met in a Vauxhall club where goggle-eyed zombies fall out on a Monday morning, donning sunglasses as they meet the rush hour commute. I was in my early twenties, he must have been nineteen. He told me he was a poet, which I found hard to believe, but I was smitten by the charming way he murmured in my ear and ran his hand under my vest. During our intense weekend together, he claimed he believed in angels. I saved him as Gabriel in my phone.

I was living abroad and, though I have a habit of turning up in wedding dresses, our dalliance didn't progress. Each time I returned to London, I quizzed the drunks in the old Soho haunts as to Gabe's actions. They were happy to buy me rum and tell me who he'd last been seen with. You missed the boat with that one, they wheezed.

The day before Christmas Eve, I returned to the same Vauxhall club. They were beginning a seven-day rave where men could pass December 25th in happy oblivion. I met a man who I'd worked with as a student: tall and willowy pretty, like a cornflower. I asked him for news of Gabe. You know he's positive, he said. He must have noticed my distress. You did use a condom, didn't you?

I spent an anxious festive period in Basingstoke. I found it harder than usual to listen to my father's philippic on my work ethic, and to lie to my grandmother that I hadn't yet found the right girl. I went first thing to the clinic in January. The tick of the clock was very loud in the waiting room as I flicked through a gay magazine with male escorts in the back pages. An advertisement said gonorrhoea was rising.

I shot up when the nurse called my name.

She peeled on latex gloves and pricked my fingertip. I watched people outside on the street below, drinking outside the Golden Lion, as she squeezed drops of my blood into a tray. What result would you be expecting today? she asked.

I don't know.

She asked me to count how many lines I saw.

Two.

That's negative.

I walked out of there as if sunshine lined my boots. I'd danced with the dragon and I hadn't yet been burnt. I had time until my evening train and I sunk a celebratory pint with Old Tom at the bar on Lisle Street. Old Tom had served in the navy and had never been able to come out. I enjoyed listening to his stories and had once accompanied him to the Union Jack club. I don't think he had any family.

One pint swiftly turned into three, and Gabe walked in with a middle-aged man, who had a silvering hairline. I cornered him while Silver was at the bar. All my anger at him faded at his cute squint. He'd been broken and I forgave him. I found myself, in a rather uncharacteristic fashion, trying to dispense wisdom.

Vauxhall is a dragon, I said, inspired by Stella Artois. You can only dance with it so often before it burns and bites.

I don't go to Vauxhall anymore.

Good. Who's the silver fox?

He's a client.

Oh right.

I didn't know what to say. He looked at his watch.

I'll be free later…

I've got to get a train.

I embraced him and went to kiss his cheek. He turned his head at the same time and I accidentally kissed the corner of his mouth.

*

I saw on Facebook that he was back in Vauxhall. I finished my *stagiaire* and found a job as an assistant at *The Literary Review* on Lexington Street. It paid pocket money but it was the dark side of the moon from gay Soho. I mostly had to sort book deliveries and occasionally somebody interesting like Michael Ondaatje would breeze into the office. I liked my colleagues though I kept reticent about my other life.

I received a message online from a man named Lee. His profile picture was of himself leaning against a BMW. He said that Gabe had asked him to contact me. Gabe was in a mental health institution in North London, if I ever wanted to visit. I asked Lee why Gabe was in an institution. He said he didn't know.

I went on to Gabe's profile and saw he hadn't posted for a month. He'd last shared an invite for a club night in Ealing. I was logging off when I saw that day, a bleak February grey, was his birthday. I mulled things over as I ripped open cardboard. He was alone on a ward on his twentieth birthday. Would anybody even visit him?

At lunchtime I went to the Tesco on Dean Street and found a card with a questionable joke about Brussel sprouts and testicles. I got on the Northern line and shakily wrote out a message with my number. By the time I located the hospital, I'd used up fifty minutes of my hour break but I figured humanity trumped the capitalist work system. The ward was separate to the main hospital and you had to cross a bridge over a babbling, Wordsworth-esque brook. A crackly intercom told me it wasn't visiting hours, but I managed to find an open window and delivered the card. I only saw the nurse's disembodied hand reaching out of the net curtain.

That evening I received a call from Gabe. It was difficult to understand him through the slurring but I ascertained he wanted me to visit. Come Saturday, I travelled the length of the Northern line again and made some good headway through *Middlemarch*, a novel I'd neglected in my undergraduate degree for the sake of cocaine. I was allowed through the first door of the Yeo Ward into a small antechamber; a uniformed nurse requested that I empty my pockets – phone, keys, wallet – into a locker. Once satisfied I was wholly dispossessed, he unlocked the second door and led me through.

There were many windows on the ward but no view. Each window looked onto a hedge, fence or carpark. Men shuffled slowly through the space staring in their own private daze. The main diagonal space had a cafeteria on the left, and a television room on the right, playing a silent football match. A corridor led to the bedrooms. The sound of banging on a door echoed through the space. No one seemed to notice.

Gabe was standing beneath a skylight. He'd put on weight, presumably on account of the medication, and was wearing a T-shirt stained with food. It seemed to take him an enormous effort to smile. We sat at a table in the cafeteria.

What happened?

Drug-induced breakdown. GHB. Mephedrone. Hadn't slept for days, paranoid, hearing voices. Risky sex. Stopped taking his HIV pills. His parents didn't know what to do. Got violent with his Dad. They phoned the police.

His fingers twitched as he spoke. I put my hands on his and a nurse reprimanded us for touching. One of the shuffling men interrupted us, as he'd heard I worked in literature and wanted me to ghost write his autobiography.

74

It was some time before he would leave. What is that banging, I asked Gabe.

Someone was acting up earlier.

Are you okay?

He shrugged. Some of the nurses are homophobic.

Is anybody else gay?

Nope.

As I was leaving, he asked me to bring him a bag of mephedrone. I've always had a live and let live attitude to drugs, but even I could tell this was a bad idea. I said no and, when the nurse was looking away, I embraced him. He relaxed into my body, as if he was exhaling pressurised breath.

*

I visited him every Saturday. I'd bring him magazines and bits of gossip from Soho. He asked me to contact friends from the scene, DJs and bar boys, and tell them he was on the ward. I wasn't sure if they ever visited. I finished the entirety of *Middlemarch* and made a start on *Anna Karenina*. Once I turned up and he'd been locked away for aggression. I wandered into the main hospital and sat before a picture of a man, his head on his palm, reading a letter. He looked unimaginably sad.

I returned home in the evening and confided in my flatmate. She was studying for a Masters in psychology and sat by the kitchen window, smoking a rollie. She asked me: do you think you're in a relationship with him?

After a month, his doctor lessened his doses. Gabe talked faster and some of his old spirit returned. Occasionally he was allowed out for supervised sojourns. He bought me a single red rose. I carried it back on the tube and thought how I'd been turned into a story. I encouraged him to engage in art therapy and he sent me the results. Reams of scrawled poetry and strange, quasi-Blake drawings arrived in the post.

He received a date for his tribunal. I booked the afternoon off work and travelled up promptly. It was held in a dimly lit staff office. Gabe was wearing an un-ironed shirt and twitching his fingers. There was just myself and an advocate from social services on his side. Three doctors sat opposite him, the three Fates spinning wool, Clotho and her sisters. They read out a long statement full of complex medical terminology. I saw the words pass over my boy's daze. He stammered through his speech.

I asked to speak. I spoke about the dragon – *it's not Vauxhall*, I said, *it's not the clubs, it's not the drugs* – and how its white-winged flight was rising over London. But they'd already woven their shroud. He was denied his release. I was asked to leave the ward as it wasn't visiting hours. Don't forget me, he said.

I sat in a cafe nearby until visiting hours. Gabe rang me from the ward payphone and asked to bring him a KFC. I queued for the takeaway still on the phone and he asked for a bucket, a zinger, chicken poppers, a mega basket. I bought it all in a XL paper bag. When I walked onto the ward, the shuffling men stared at the banquet. One by one they began a slow chant of *Ba - tty - boys, ba - tty - boys.*

Gabe shouted for them to stop. They only chanted louder. Male nurses appeared and he backed into a corner, his fists raised. Before they could grab him, I went and touched his shoulders. His vision focussed on me and he dropped his fists. I wanted to embrace him but I feared they'd ask me to leave again.

I stopped at the stream that evening, watching its waters. Freedom is not an essence, it's given by those who surround us. On the train back to Blackfriars, I couldn't concentrate on my book. For all his beauty of humanity, Tolstoy didn't write about myself or Gabe. The dragon is an appetite, you see, the dragon is a mirror to the mind, it lives and feeds inside. It's a smoke shape drifting through men's minds, crafted by familial embarrassment, by the yelling of *queer* in schools, by the intrinsic moral evil of religion. The world has always spoken in violence to Gabe.

I walked across Blackfriars bridge, the cold April sun setting on the Thames, surrounded by the rush hour commuters. On the Southern side I leant my head in my arm and wept against a building, as the crowd broke and flowed around me. There's not a one of us in this life not laced with madness.

London Independent Story Prize 2nd Round Finalist

Tony Warner

'The children will be late for school.'

Once the carer had left he settled into the normal routine. He propped Alice up in her chair where she sat singing to herself, turning her bracelets round and round on her wrists. The reflection from the coloured glass fractured the pale walls like transient rainbows. 'The children will be late for school,' she said.

He did not reply. He had long since given up telling her the children had left home thirty years ago, in the time of her exuberant health. Or perhaps she meant the grandchildren, who never came any more, frightened of the old witch in the armchair.

The lid of the kettle rattled, causing him to turn from the sink and pour the water in the pot. Breakfast was the only meal he enjoyed. Alice was calm after a long night's sleep and often clean and dry. The new carer was good and efficient, not like many of the others, washing Alice down, making sure she had emptied her bowels, dressing her in warm, sensible clothes. Others left her to stink for days or weeks, threw on any old rags. Getting anyone to come out here into the country was difficult. They made excuses: the lane off the road could not be found, the rains made it impassable, the extra travelling time made their schedule impossible.

He stirred the porridge in Alice's bowl, adding a generous swirl of honey. Honey from their own bees. Only one hive now he was on his own with her to look after. One had died off last summer, the victim of varroa or the poison the farmer spread on his fields. If the last hive failed to survive this year he would give up on the bees as he had given up on most of the garden. The strawberries looked after themselves, the gooseberries thrived but potatoes and carrots were hard work; hard digging for both planting and harvesting. Besides, they ate almost nothing and the carer brought the little he had on regular order from the shop in the village.

'The children will be late for school,' said Alice again.

'They left a minute ago,' he said. 'Look, they left their porridge again. We'll have to finish it ourselves, as always.'

'As always,' she repeated.

He sat next to her, spooning small amounts into her mouth. Last year she was able to feed herself. Now she had neither the desire nor the coordination, as with all her food. He made her soft meals, ones which required no cutting or chewing, catching half masticated gobbets from the side of her mouth with a spoon, re-feeding them as one does with a baby. There was no need with the porridge, sliding down easily, lubricated by the honey.

'The children will be late for school,' she said.

'They left ages ago, my darling, See, they finished all of their breakfast. Aren't they good children?'

She subsided, humming more tunes from their shared youth. 'Hey, wait a minute Mr. Postman.' 'Has the postman been?' She asked suddenly. 'Maybe Max has sent us a letter.' Max, who was away in Australia, who never called or wrote. Max, who she had fussed and worried over, forgiving all his faults and transgressions, even when they had had to denude their meagre savings to rescue him from prison. Max never called or wrote.

'Has the postman been?' she asked again.

He said nothing. Washed up the breakfast things in the sink, gazing at the leaves of the beech trees in the far copse, gently turning ochre in the autumn breeze. Winter will be here soon, he thought, closing down their world, trapping them ever more firmly indoors, buffeted by the winds, enslaved by the cold. How much oil was left in the tank? Did he have enough money to fill it up? The company would not deliver a half load. Every year they were less amenable to negotiating the narrow lane, every year the oil was more and more expensive. It was beautiful, though, the autumn, the sycamores and the oaks turning the colour of Alice's hair in the sunlight. A muddy winter brown now, streaked with white icicles.

'The children will be late for school,' she said.

He sighed. Fetched the shoe box from under the settee, placed it on Alice's lap. Once upon a time the photographs had been neatly collated in envelopes held tight with rubber bands. Now they were all bent and dog-eared, eras and places mixed promiscuously in a jumble of half-memories.

Alice picked through them at random, a puzzled look on her face, turning them over to see what was written on the back. Those she failed to recognise she let drop to the floor beside her chair. Every day the pile he had to gather up grew larger.

80

They sat companionably together. She fumbled through her photographs. He watched her, sipping at his cold tea, fumbling through his memories. There was no post.

The shoe box was almost empty. Alice picked out a photograph. Larger than most of the others. She squinted at it, held it at arms' length, turned it over to see if there was any writing on the back. Stared at it for what he felt to be an age.

'Who is this?' she asked. 'Look at his long hair and tight trousers. Very handsome. And she is so beautiful. I don't remember them. Who can they be? Why don't I remember them?'

'Don't fret yourself, my darling. Dry your eyes. Look at them together. Here is grandma's old cottage. Do you remember the cherry trees? And this is us, the day we told everyone we were getting married. We were beautiful together. Don't you remember? We couldn't get enough of one another, all over one another.'

'The children will be late for school.' She dropped the photograph on the floor along with the others.

He sighed. Made his way unsteadily into the kitchen. Unlocked the bottom drawer of the dresser; reached inside for the key. Tucked it into his trouser pocket.

'Time for bed, my darling,' he said, stretching out his arms.

'Still light,' she said.

'The time of the year, my sweet. Midsummer. See, the sun is shining, the leaves are on the trees.'

'The children,' she said.

'With grandma. They always stay with grandma in the summer.'

'Yes,' she said, making an effort to rise.

He helped her to her feet, gave her his arm to rest on. She smiled.

He helped her up the narrow stairs. Stood her on the landing, brushed her hair, flowing down to her waist in still abundant curls. Carefully he undressed her, piece by piece: pullover, top, skirt, cotton pants, thick woollen socks, folding each neatly and stacking them on the chair next to the bed. He pulled back the bedclothes, steering her beneath the covers, where she lay rigid.

Just as carefully and neatly, he undressed himself, laying out the clothes on his side of the bed. Instead of entering from his side, he turned to hers, gently pulled back the covers. She shivered. He eased her legs apart, inserted his head between them, licked at the dry lips of her vagina, first down one side, then the other. She relaxed, muttered something he could not hear, moved gently, stroked his naked shoulder.

His member remained flaccid, unwilling to carry congress further, unused over fallow years to the primordial exercise. Seeking for inspiration, he conjured up the photograph, the pair of them on the steps of grandma's cottage in the days of their unrestrained youth. Within seconds he hardened, rising to full height and strength. Wary of losing the erection, he moved swiftly, entering her smoothly and gently.

She remained immobile. He moved slowly, a gentle rhythm. A movement of her legs, catching at his; she caught his hair in her hand, gradually joining him as he thrust faster and deeper, hesitant fingers playing a light glissando along his back. He kissed her fleetingly, as a swallow dives to sip from a flowing stream, held himself as close within as he dare. She whimpered, let out a cry. Then a groan, a rattle like ancient machinery grinding to a final halt.

They rested. He leant back to his side of the bed. She turned on her side to face him. Closed her eyes. 'The children,' she said, 'the children.'

He kissed her once more. Got up, pissed in the old stained toilet. Fetched the key from his trouser pocket, went naked downstairs to the cellar. Opened the cupboard, left it ajar. He had imagined this in his mind many times before, ever putting off the moment. In his imagination it had come to him as a dark day in winter, cold and snow outside. Now, the autumn sunshine seemed more appropriate. He paused a few moments to write some lines which he left on the kitchen table.

There was nothing left to chance, all had been rehearsed several times over the preceding years. The cartridges were medium sized shot, good for rabbits, too heavy for pheasants and grouse. He loaded one for each barrel, lay the gun along the line of the pillow.

'The children,' she said. 'The children.'

He fired once. Her beauty disappeared in a mass of blood and tissue. He turned away. Lay on his back with the barrel of the shotgun beneath his chin. A rifle was no use, the bullet could pass all the way through with no fatal damage. Shotgun pellets spread like a broken glass on a stone floor.

He wedged his toe under the trigger guard. 'The children will be late for school,' he said.

London Independent Story Prize 3ʳᵈ Round Finalist

Jean Roarty

Always Her Best Girls

At the Nursing Home door, a single leaf pirouettes downward landing on my shoe. I stare at the golden corpse of what was once summer, then stab in the door code. Margaret is on reception today.

'Hi, Deirdre,' she says.

All the staff know me. I've been coming here for years. Since Mother's admission, a host of residents have died. Whenever they say so and so *passed away,* I always wonder why they can't say died. At times a pang of envy hits me and I indulge in thoughts of the deliverance Mother's death would bring.

The visitor's book lies open on the desk: *Visitor's Name, Resident's Name, Time In, Time Out.* I no longer write Mother's name. She is number 42. The clock on the wall says 11.30, but I write 11.25, always shaving a few minutes on the way in, then adding a few minutes on the way out. I will be glad in an hour, when, if it's a good day, I'll wheel Mother to the dining room and escape. I brace myself before heading down the long corridor to her room. Unanswered call bells ring incessantly. The corridor bends around to the right where a wall of glass lets in a flood of early autumn light. I watch dead leaves, whorl into mini tornadoes, then quiver as the wind eases. The leaves gather in a heap in one spot of the flower bed, the way dust favours one corner of my hall.

My heart lightens when I peep inside the room. No sign of Mother. The days when she's bedbound due to illness, spinal fractures and pressure sores are the worst.

Her pain is my pain.

When she first got ill I promised, if things got bad, I'd help her to die even if it meant going to jail. Ever since, we refer to our little pact as 'the tablet'. That plan helped her to live. My sisters have always known about my promise to Mother.

I hasten to the Day Room. Amongst the lines of elderly men and women I see Mother's slumped body—a white-haired shell, trapped in her wheelchair. I go over and hug her bony frame. Her sunken eyes sparkle.

'I'm so glad you came, Deirdre. She has slid down in the wheelchair. Two people are needed to lift her back up.

'We'll get you straightened up, go to your room and have a nice cup of tea.'

On the far side of the room, I spot her friend, Janette, and wave to her. Mother's arms are weak, but she can manage to propel her wheelchair slowly. When she's confused or overwhelmed by pain and powerlessness, she ends up in Janette's room. Janette looks out for her. When I bring in mint sweets, I leave a second packet inside Janette's door.

'Hang on a sec, Mother,' I let go of the wheelchair's ridged handles and make my way over to Janette, kneeling in front of her to say a quick hello.

'Pull over that chair,' she says, gesturing towards an empty one.

'I can't stay, Mother is waiting.'

Janette sighs, a frown crossing her face. She leans forward. 'Just to let you know,' she says. 'Your mother's gone off mints.'

'Oh, has she?'

'Yes. Maybe bring in jellies for a change.'

In my peripheral vision I see Mother trying to move her wheelchair as if asking to leave, as if not wanting to share me. 'Sorry Janette, I have to go. Thanks for the heads-up about the sweets.'

Before I get to Mother, she has already crashed into Jim's armchair. He doesn't notice. I manoeuvre her out and we go to her room. We park the wheelchair in the usual spot—near the door and within reach of the little shelf unit. She likes the door left open, through which the muffled sounds of the Day Room TV can be heard. I rearrange items on the shelf to make room for the tray, move the jewellery-draped Statue of Liberty back against the wall, and shove the dusty glasses case, sticky protein drink and kidney-shaped sick bowl out of the way.

'Are you warm enough?' Her red nylon blouse looks a little flimsy. 'Will I get you a cardigan?'

'I'm okay.' The blouse clashes with her faded purple skirt. The yellow knee socks aren't hers.

There's not much furniture in her room apart from a small table with a framed photo of us three as children, on it. The photo is angled so it can be seen from the bed. The floor space is taken up with the hoist, lumber roll, blue plastic body pillow and other paraphernalia. Her rigid legs, like locked hinges, fall awkwardly to one side, and her feet hang off the footrests. I reposition her legs and force her feet into place, careful of the broken skin that bleeds like ketchup from her heels. A lifetime ago, those feet danced their way to an All-Ireland Ballroom title.

I place the cup of tea in her good hand. 'There you go.' She tries to take a sip. The cup lists in her hand.

'Watch out,' I shout. Some tea sloshes out over the side of the cup.

'I'm such a messer.' As she tries to smile, immutable pain is engraved on her face. At the next attempt, she manages to take a drink without spilling the tea. Usually, it falls on the floor in a puddle. If we use a straw, it wobbles towards her pursed lips and cartwheels into her lap. A beaker is easier for her to manage, but she doesn't like the taste of plastic. She clasps the white cup with both hands now. As a child, I used to marvel at her painted nails, longing to become like her. I remember those hands clasped in pleading prayer, despite her not being in the slightest bit religious.

'Like one of these?' I show Mother the little catering pack of digestive biscuits that she is unable to open herself. She shakes her head, then jiggles her left hand before attempting another sip of tea. A metallic Medic-Alert bracelet dangles on her wrist since her stint in Intensive Care with anaphylactic shock. She is allergic to penicillin. Even the smallest dose would be fatal.

It's easy to order penicillin online without a prescription. I have a supply at home. It stays in date for three years. I keep it renewed.

'What day is it today, Deirdre?'

'Friday.'

I pour more tea. Realising how hungry I am, I reach for the biscuits and hear her whisper, 'I wish I was dead.'

'I know you do.' She wants, as Oscar Wilde put it, to *forget time, to forgive life, to be at peace.*

'What age am I?'

'Seventy-nine.'

'Am I really? What day is it today, Deirdre?'

'Still Friday.'

She manages a faint smile. She is in so much pain she can't talk.

'It's my back.' She tries to move. Unable to adjust her body, there is no relief.

For the next while Mother lies in bed, too ill to be hoisted out. My sisters and I spend as much time as we can at her bedside. When she asks for 'the tablet', I know what she means and agree to bring in the penicillin the following morning. Our understanding is such nothing more needs to be said. Now the time is here, it's scarier than I'd anticipated.

When Mother drifts into a kind of sleep, Kate, my oldest sister, says 'We need to talk. Let's get a coffee from the kitchen and have it in the library.' The library is a room at the end of the corridor that's usually empty. It has a shelf with a few books on it, and a computer. The odd time you might see a resident, accompanied by a Care Assistant, using the computer.

Kate places her coffee on the little table. 'The palliative team can't do any more. I was on to them again. You'd think in this day and age–'

'I'm bringing the penicillin in with me in the morning,' I inform them.

None of us speak.

'There'll be a postmortem,' says Caroline, breaking the silence. 'You'll go to jail. Your Jenny's only fourteen.' She gets up and goes over to the door. 'Will I close it?'

'Better not, they like it kept open.'

'What if it doesn't work?'

'It will work. She can't be any worse.'

Caroline massages her temples. 'In this country it's considered murder.'

'Well, it shouldn't be.' I take a sip of coffee, too stressed to let my anger surface.

'You'll go to jail,' Caroline adds. Kate nods in agreement.

'You think I don't know that? You two don't have—
'

Kate stands up. 'We'd better go back. Don't do anything 'til we are all here.'

'How are things?' I ask as I enter Mother's room the following morning, armed with the medicine.

'Terrible,' Caroline says. 'She's had enough; she wants to go. If I'd had the penicillin last night, I'd have given it to her myself.'

As soon as Kate arrives, Caroline closes the door. It doesn't lock, for health and safety reasons. We sit in silence around the bed, frozen with apprehension. Mother looks tiny. Her legs lie bent underneath the white sheet as though half of her is missing. We have a small window of opportunity to give her the penicillin before the staff come in to turn her.

From my handbag I pull out the zip-lock bag filled with yellow-and-red capsules. Mother is positioned upright, her hands resting on the steel safety bars. She watches as I empty the powder from about twelve capsules into the beaker and stir in some water.

'Thank you,' she whispers.

'Remember when you got the cannabis, thinking it would help your legs to move?' Kate says, holding Mother's hand. 'You hid the tinfoil packages in with your Oxo cubes, remember?

I join in. 'And the way we'd dance around the kitchen.' I place the beaker on the shelf and dance with an imaginary partner in the narrow space between the table and the wall. 'Slow slow, quick quick, slow. Slow slow, quick—
'

The framed photo crashes to the floor, jolting us back to the task in hand. Kate hands the poisoned cup to me. The enormity of what we are doing reduced to a plastic beaker. Watched by Mother, Kate hurriedly gathers up the remaining capsules and discarded shells and shoves them

90

into her handbag. When I ask Caroline to guard the door, I see the fear in her eyes. I hold the beaker towards Mother's pursed lips. It trembles in my hand. She forces her head towards the drink.

'Under the bed,' she says. We look at one another and shrug.

'Always my best girls,' she adds. I gently pour the liquid into her mouth. She manages to swallow it, pauses, opens her mouth for more, then bravely gulps the rest. She lies back and closes her eyes. Her face turns red, then white like ivory. Her breath comes from her throat and stops.

'She's gone,' Kate murmurs.

An emptiness descends on the room.

We look at one another. Reality hits. Tears haemorrhage. The beaker feels like a grenade in my hand. Better rinse it out. On my way to the bathroom, a dropped yellow-and-red capsule glints up at me from under the bed. Wow!

Laid out in her room, Mother lies still like a beautiful doll. Her olive-green dress is missing a button. It is so strange to see her legs straight. They must have broken them. We stay with her for ages. I expect her to respond when I kiss her forehead, to ask how old she is, what day is it today.

We make our way out to the car park. It is an ordinary day for everyone else. The pathway is strewn with brittle leaves that once clothed the trees.

London Independent Story Prize 3rd Round Finalist Anne Wilkins

Aroha

I live in clean, green, New Zealand — I think of this as Granny and I watch plastic shit float out to the sea.

I hear her give her little tut, tuts under her breath. She holds my hand for support, as we walk together by the shoreline. Granny must be like a hundred. No one knows her exact age, but she's as old as a Kauri tree. Her face looks like it's covered in cobwebs, and her eyes are so hooded that they droop on her face. She gives my hand a little squeeze; it means she loves me, and I squeeze back and I remind myself to wash my hands when we get back to the house.

"You okay, Aroha?"

"Yeah." I'm not okay, but I don't wanna talk about it, none of it. I'd rather look at the shit in the ocean, and wish it were my shit drifting away, far away, so far that it couldn't hurt me no more.

"Your Mother's still with you, yeah. In here." Granny thumps her breastbone.

"I know." I don't wanna say any more in case the tears come again. I know my Mama's inside of me, cos that's where I feel the pain the most. Like I've been stabbed or something. But it just must be Mama making room for herself inside of me.

I look down at the sand. There's so much of it. Tiny little grains, broken down. Broken.

"We're gonna look after each other, you and I. You think you're up to it, girl?" Granny gives me a look. I'd never thought about me looking after Granny, I'd always thought Granny would be the one looking after me.

Maybe Granny needs me, I think, as much as I need her. "I'll look after you, Granny." I squeeze her hand. She gives me a long, slow smile, like the sun slowly coming up, but it's worth it, as it makes it all the way to her eyes.

"We'll be a good team, you and I. Just you see." She gives me a big hug. "Ah, my little mokopuna," she says. She cradles me like Mama once did and strokes my long hair. I tell myself I'll need to shower as soon as we get home.

Mama and I were once a team, we did everything together. No dad in the picture, so just me and Ma. She'd named me Aroha, cos' it means love in Māori, *and you've got so much love in your heart baby girl, so much love.* She'd give me big hugs, like Granny, but back then I didn't wash the hugs off. I just leaned into them, sorta inhaled them. I didn't know I was killing Mama.

They tell me it's not my fault that she died, but I know that ain't true. It was me that got sick first. *Bad flu,* they said. Mama gave me lemon drinks and manuka honey, and I bounced right back. Then it was her turn with it, like we were playing tag or something, but with being sick. *Your turn Mama.* But it wasn't no game, and Mama didn't bounce back like me. She got so pale, and it was hard for her to breathe in the end.

I gave her the lemons and the honey, just like she'd given me, but she stayed on the couch, not moving much. Some days she'd burn so hot, and others she shivered real bad.

Granny says Mama should've called for help, but Mama was always proud like that, she didn't need no help, and besides she had me, I was her team. But I wasn't a good person to have in your team, I'm like the kid who's super slow or something, the one you hope the teacher doesn't put you with. I was that kid, and I was killing Mama.

It was me that called 111 in the end. They'd asked me what I wanted, fire, police, ambulance, and I'd just cried and said my Mama was sick and I couldn't wake her up. She wasn't dead then, but she died later, in the hospital. Everyone was surprised cos Mama had been so fit. Granny had stood beside the hospital bed, and given her little tut tuts, and had held my hand.

They'd had a big whanau (family) meeting with some white people about me. I never knew I had so much family. I was told it was Granny who put her hand up for me the longest and the hardest. I don't know why she wanted me so bad, given how old she was, but I guess she didn't know I'd killed Mama.

When we make it back to the house, I go inside and wash my hands over and over again. But it's still not enough. I'll have Granny's germs all over me, from the hug, from her stroking my hair. I run the shower. It's not like the one Mama had, it's older, and Granny says they're on tank water. I turn it up to hot and just let the water boil my skin. Killing whatever's on me. I've got to get it off, all of it. I lather myself with soap, and scrub my hair with shampoo. *"Hair like tūī's feathers Aroha. Beautiful,"* my Mama used to say. I don't have that hair no more. If Mama were around still she'd tell me my hair was like a possum's bum. Anyway, it don't matter, she's not around.

I turn the taps off, and just stand there. Finally I feel clean. And empty. And broken.

When I come out of the shower a trail of steam follows me. I wrap myself in a towel and open the door. Granny is standing right outside, she looks cross. "Aroha, you're gonna use all our water at this rate!"

"Won't the tank fill up with the rain?'

94

"Not the rate you're using it at. Didn't you just have a shower yesterday?"

"I felt dirty."

"Dirty? From what?"

From you. From the hug. From your hands. I shrug my shoulders, "I dunno."

"What're we gonna do with you? We gotta get rid of some of these big city ways eh?" She says this affectionately, but I'm hurt. "Go, get dressed girl, and we'll get some kai ready for dinner, eh?"

I trundle down the hall to my bedroom. There's no carpet here, just wooden floorboards, Granny says the floorboards are rimu. They dent and scratch easily, and there's a ton of little holes and cracks where bad stuff can breed. I walk carefully, trying to mind the splits in the wood.

My bedroom's real nice. My Mama used to sleep here. I think I can smell her here. Sometimes it's so nice, it makes me wanna cry and I hug my pillow like I'm hugging my Mama. From my window I can see the sea. There's no plastic at this distance, that's good, everything is better at a distance.

I get dressed and I help Granny with dinner. It's been a week now, so I kinda know what to do, the veges to get, the food to chop. She grows a lot of the veges herself, kumara, lettuce, broccoli, spinach, yams (which I'd never had before). She's also got a lot of fruit too: mandarins (they're not out yet), apples - some with yucky holes in them, grapefruit and lemons.

It's a lot for Granny to look after and she has help. I've got uncles and aunties nearby who're always stopping in, and cousins too. I know Granny says we're a team, but I'm glad she's got other people in her team too. I like it best though when it's just me and Granny, and she tells me stories about Mama. Like the time Mama climbed a tree and couldn't get down, or how she used to swim like an ika in the sea, faster than her brothers even though she was smaller. The old stories make me smile, and Mama must like them too, cos' it grows warm inside me.

Tonight we're eating fish caught by my uncle with some potato all mashed up. There's beans and peas too, which don't taste too bad when you mix them up in all the potato.

"We gotta talk, Aroha." It sounds bad when Granny says things like this.

"Uh-huh." I look down at my plate and shovel the food in my mouth.

"You're cleaning yourself so much you're gonna make yourself sick."

"That don't make sense, Granny."

"Āe, it does. You're washing all the goodness away. What are you trying to do girl, wash away bad memories?"

"No."

"Then what is it?"

It's the bad things. The germs. The things that make you sick. They're everywhere, on you Nana. On me. Everywhere. If you don't get rid of them, someone's gonna die.

"I just feel dirty, that's all."

Granny sighs. "You heard of Papatūānuku?"

Granny was always on about the old myths and legends. I didn't know much, but I knew a little from what I'd been taught at school. "You mean the Earth mother?"

"Yeah. That's the one. You think she's happy with all that plastic we saw today?"

"No."

"We gotta do things good for the Earth. Do what we can."

"What's that gotta do with having showers?"

96

"Cos what you're doing is no good for the Earth. You're having showers every day, for half an hour, you're on your second shampoo bottle, and burning through the hot water like we got plenty to spare. You're gonna make me broke if you keep going like this."

I feel the familiar sting in my eyes as I listen to her words. I stare down at the table.

"You shine child, always have. Blue-black hair, just like your Mama, but you wash all that shine away."

The picture of my Mama is so sharp and sudden it's like a slap in the face. I put down my knife and fork. I can't eat. Something's stuck in there, not food, but I can't swallow. Words manage to push their way out though. "You don't have to have me, I can go back to Auckland," I blurt.

Granny talks soft this time, "Child, I want you to live here with me. But we gotta start making some changes. Good changes."

I look at my kuia. She looks so sad, the sun I saw earlier in her eyes is setting. She doesn't understand, none of it. She just sees a stupid girl wasting water. And all I see is the bad things, everywhere, the germs crawling over all of us. Crawling over Granny, feasting on her. I don't like talking about bad things in case they come true, so I whisper, "...I don't wanna get sick again Granny. And I don't want you to get sick."

"Sweetheart, is that what this is all about?"

I give a slow nod. It's too much to do anything else as I feel I might turn to mush, like my potato.

Granny gets up from where she's been sitting and wraps me in her arms. She holds me close, while I let out little sobs.

"I killed Mama," I finally admit aloud. My words are muffled against her chest, but it feels good to set them free.

"Is that what you think? Is that what this is all about?"

I give a little nod.

Granny pulls me away so she can look me in the eyes, "You did no such thing child. It was your Mama's time that's all. We all have a time, and that was hers. Your Mama had a big heart, too big, that made her sicker, not you."

"That true?"

"Would I lie to you?"

I shake my head. Granny's all about honesty.

"You know," she continues, "We all get sick, and showering all the time is not gonna stop you getting sick. You'll be washing yourself so much there'll be nothing left but a little blob of a girl."

I make a strange sound, it's half sob, half laugh. She ruffles my hair. My wild mess of a hair.

"Aroha, your Granny knows things. And I reckon we're gonna be alright me and you."

"You think so?"

"I know so."

I've got Granny all over me. In my hair, on my arms, even on my cheek. But this time I'm not thinking of washing her away.

"I love you, Granny."

"E aroha hoki ahau i a koe."

She pulls me in for another hug, so close, so tight, that I feel Mama right there with us, moving inside my heart.

The End

London Independent Story Prize 3rd Round Finalist

Erini Loucaides

The Roots of Things

If she calls you 'slut', you will imagine yourself a photon, travelling at the speed of light, too fast for the word to attach itself to you. And you've been surprisingly reassured to discover that 'whore' is derived from the Old English *hōre* which in turn is rooted in the Proto-Indo-European *kéhros*, meaning 'loved'. Where did it go wrong? At what point did the twisting vines of history spin 'whore' one-hundred-and-eighty degrees?

It's hard to imagine the woman seated in the first pine wood pew calling you 'slut' or 'whore' but a tailored beige suit and praying beneath the large figure of Christ on a blue-blue cross are no guarantee.

The Higgs field penetrates every region of the universe. It continually interacts with elementary particles, giving them mass.

The sun streaming through the jewelled glass windows (you hate the word 'stained') on this early autumn morning feels like cardigan on your skin. His funeral service was held here, the one you didn't attend, but this is the first time you've entered the church.

You do not belong here, this is not yours. Yet, it is appropriate for your confession. To her.

99

Your steel yourself for approach, to tell her you'd like a word, many words stored like the tightly packed force inside an atom.

Months ago, you'd set the stage, seemingly bumping into her along the dairy aisle of Waitrose. She had mistaken you for a waitress, a Fabiana working at some Italian. You corrected her, revealed your occupation but not your name, scrutinising her face for recognition — perhaps he'd mentioned the interior designer?— but her face remained courteous, her smile congealed at the same width.

An electron spins in the Higgs field until a mass is added to it whereupon it is changed, spinning in the opposite direction.

Now is the time to move towards her but your boots feel rooted to the encaustic tiles. You know why. The mass of what you will foist upon her, that extra particle, will convert this church into a Higgs field forcing her to spin in a different direction, forever changed.

*

With a name like Peter Higgs, of course there were others: the band, the German shepherd, an Aussie surfer and the Scottish, Nobel-lauded physicist you kept stumbling upon. You didn't click on the physicist's pages, not that first time, that dominoed later.

On Instagram, there he was, Peter Higgs of Deloitte, your new client. There was a gravitational pull even from the screen, before your first meeting. His features were unremarkable in and of themselves: thin lips, large striding nose and dated cow-lick hair. Of course, you of all people, know well how plain objects and furniture arranged with symmetry and startling contrast birth quantum allure.

That night, two hours, maybe more, sitting in your apartment, smoking White Slims and scrolling through what he wanted the world to take in: meetings in Vienna, canoeing in the Dordogne Valley, seafood dinners in Cape Town. Out of the hundred or so pictures, three with his wife, blue-blue skies behind them. Vera Higgs: bobbed, thin in jeans and flowing scarves. Smiles-smiles.

So, you knew when you met to discuss his office vision of 'neutrals with splashes of coral', seated at Abu Danys scooping falafels, you knew. And had he scrolled through @DHatzyInteriors to view the country house in Englefield Green or the converted church whose owner had hired you on the spot when she found out you'd done a Feng Shui course in Singapore?

Over the next few meetings, you seized opportunities to rake him over: the uneven smile veering left, the ripples on his forehead every time he raised his eyebrows, the hooded and unnervingly deep-set eyes like caves of flint, the shadow of stubble coalescing into a triangle between his lower lip and chin. From the collar of his crisp Armani shirts, a small solid gold cross (gift from her?) peeked out when he leaned over your MacBook Pro. But it was the Cartier band on his ring finger you hated. You've never liked that symbol, circle with a line right through it. No entry, no go, forbidden. It didn't stop you though, did it?

The Higgs field is remarkably unique possessing spin 0. Gravity though, does have a spin and can be defined as being a part of space and time.

When you began the sex, (by the sixth meeting, by the fourth Mojito), there was no time continuum, or if there was, you floated away from it, temporarily, voluntarily, a passing particle excited at this new expanse, heavily captured in it like an almond dropped in a pool of honey.

One languid morning, you playfully told him about his Nobel namesake. In response, he nuzzled your Achilles heel located in the dip of your left shoulder and murmured, 'Fuck his field. You're in my one now, Hatzy'.

Dora Hatzy. Pruned from Theodoritsa Hatzigiorkatzi, a messy mass of a name, grafted from po-faced Greek saints and ancestral pilgrimages.

And 'Higgs'. Gaelic, from 'Mac Aodha' 'son of Aodh' Celtic god of fire.

Higgy and Hatzy, you would whisper to yourself, but never to him. So cute yet, in reality, so very crude, so crude you couldn't confess it to *Pater* Demetrius' in his oak-wood confessional booth that summer in Athens.

More than once, when Peter was fiddling with the hook of your bra or tugging at the zip of your black trousers, you reached up and fingered his cross.

'How can you wear that, when we do what we do?'

'Shush.'

'But how can you?'

'For Christ's sake Hatz, talk about timing.'

You had all the warning flares with reactions like that (and you hated him dropping the Y in your name). Moments when you should have spliced the mistress from the interior designer and left the hotel where the lift took you from the dark underground parking lot right up to the room. 'Custom built for us outlaws, he'd laugh, my buddy owns it so we're good'.

It's harder for a particle to change the direction of its spin the quicker it vibrates.

But like a million other mistresses before you and a million more to come, you gave in to him tugging the cotton crotch of your panties to one side.

Nights were never yours. Afternoons and some mid mornings, was all. Scrolling nights. And when Peter Higgs, the physicist, kept orbiting your searches, you clicked on new fields. Maybe because atoms, with their quarks, electrons, protons and neutrons are the ultimate interior design. In many photos, the physicist stood in front of his whiteboard flowing with arrows and asterisks and half the Greek alphabet, as if he'd worked out the physics of your relationship, the warning maths.

The Greek word for adultery, μοχεία, is generous to you for it is defined as the seduction of a free woman by a married man. But in English, with crystallising dismay, you saw that it applied to you too, not just the married party.

ADULT. ER. ER.

Adult. Err. Err.

Takes 2.

$$E = mc^2$$

Excitement = magnetic coitus squared (Latin, past participle of coire, 'to come together').

But the Higgs field was too honeyed and you didn't want to wade out.

Photons are weightless. They flow at the speed of light, their torque unaffected by the Higgs field, not subject to oscillations, and moving right through the field.

One afternoon she called as you were unbuttoning the tiny pearls of your shirt, and he, seated on the side of the quilted silk bed, still dressed. His hand, the one with the Cartier ring, moved in rigid left and right motions, a windshield wiper cleaning you away.

You masked your stab wound, your desiccation, with spasmodic nods and a shaky smile. Good mistress, button up and leave. The shiny hotel doorknob threw your gnarled reflection back at you, prickly-pear nose and drooping eyes, a Mediterranean goblin. Before you blotted it out with your grip, her deep cry surrounded the room through his i-Phone: 'Embryos failed . . . no more . . . no sixth time, Peter'.

You gave him space, good mistress, throwing yourself full time into the time-space continuum of gravity, timetables and deadlines.

Two weeks later, your first messages. Work-related and never sent at night but still, he was ghosting you.

Dark energy backbones the universe, dark energy breathes expansion, a massive black hole is at the heart of every galaxy; an attosecond is a billionth of a billionth second and changes in electrons happen in tenths of an attosecond.

He'd ghosted you all. Gone in an attosecond.

Tagged by Vera. Her single photo, their honeymoon in Thailand clinking cocktails with little pink umbrellas captioned, *I know you'll light up heaven the way you lit up my life.*

Aneurysm.

Your mind sought to break it down in those immediate moments, inside pulsars of shock.

Neurysm

A = στεριτικο αλφα (alpha privative, Google translated).

Neurysm = νευρο, his nerves betrayed him.

An artery, Google corrected, not a nerve, that bulged, burst and bled.

For days on end, you wanted nicotine in your lungs to stop you floating into empty space. But you tried not to and instead took to string cheese, half-eaten on your plat, moulding. Decay was better than emptiness. Decay required growth.

And echoing words became haunterers in the growing months.

Aneurysm/A new reason.

*

You must tell her. It is unfair not to, you have convinced yourself as you gaze up at Christ on the blue-blue cross. She needs to know she has a grandchild. Her son lives on.

Observing alters the behaviour of the particle being observed due to the wave-like nature of matter.

She shuffles, ill at ease, turns back to the front, hastily crossing herself then rising. Is her sudden awareness of your presence the cause of her change in behaviour? Would she have prayed longer? Wept?

You have long set the safety nets for 'slut' and 'whore' but you suddenly realise verbs will tear through those safety nets.

You destroyed

You ruined

You wrecked

And beginnings like *Because of you . . .*

They will pierce your nucleus. How will you brace yourself for the implosion? And had he confided in her after you'd sent him that last cliché sms, two days before the aneurysm?

Peter, pls answer

106

Urgent.

Something you must know

She adjusts her handbag, keeps her head down as she taps down the low steps. The torque of your heart intensifies, your lips uproot. Her perfume is old feminine cologne.

'Mrs Higgs?'

'Yes?'

'We meet again.'

'Do we?'

'From the supermarket, remember?'

You heart bellyflops in your chest when her phone rings just as you've found your momentum. She fumbles, pearlescent nail polish. You gesture, move your mouth, probably too Mediterranean-like, signalling you will wait. She blinks rapidly, moves away, leaning against the second last pew.

It gives you time to study her in a way you couldn't in the supermarket. He'd told you that his father had fallen for her because she resembled Charlotte Rampling. You'd had no idea who Charlotte Rampling was but Google showed the similarity in the intense hooded gaze, the curvature and fullness of her lips.

She ends her call, glances uncertainly at you, then checks her handbag in that obsessive-compulsive manner you've seen before. Her parting words are raspy.

'Excuse me, my daughter-in-law is arriving.'

*

The dark headstone isn't Nabresina like the other graves. His is black marble with gold engraving, *Gone too soon to light up heaven.*

The sixth visit. You couldn't at first, fearing this deadness was bad Feng Shui for the baby. Even after her birth, you still couldn't.

Always a weekday, after sunset, not long before closing, is when you go. You place different flowers every time. Today's it's hypericum berries. Hyper. Ikon. Hanging over icons.

You hadn't intended to bring Laura, not yet, but the nanny cancelled last minute and you took it as a sign that perhaps now was a good time for her mind to imprint images. In the years to come, you will need to tightrope between truth and appropriateness.

Beside you, in her miniature jeans and jumper, she is whining for a hypericum stalk. You pluck one from the vase but she shakes her head, her little flesh-dough hand reaching up and closing over the largest cluster.

'Just like your daddy, wanting the biggest slice,' you playfully whisper as if the dead around you might hear.

You hand her the stalk, keeping an eye to ensure she doesn't attempt to eat the berries. You will take them off her the moment her attention is seized by something else, usually the grave beside his with its two huge praying angels.

Entanglement is the intrinsic connection between two or more quantum particles offering the possibility of correlation. Einstein called Entanglement 'spooky action at a distance'.

The air is condensing. It won't be long before the sky turns lapis lazuli and night stretches into you.

He has widened, a mass of phantom photons changing the Feng Shui of the London skies.

Is how you like to imagine him.

You take her left hand, the berries are in her right. You shuffle up the concrete, through the graves, through times and names.

Given the late hour you are surprised at the soft voices from beyond the metal gates. A petite woman pushing an older one in a wheelchair emerge as one unit and you begin unravelling like a ball of yarn when Laura pulls it apart.

Your mind thrashes for safety nets.

We are all just atoms, no, we are the spaces between the atoms, between the protons and neutrons, unaffected by the Higgs field. Particles have shown they can bounce backwards, going backwards in time —

But it won't be spliced into its smaller components and you are forced to look at it in all its largeness and fullness and fleshness.

Vera. Woman of Thai honeymoon, of smiles-smiles, of flat belly and floating scarves. She's moving, no longer a frozen one-dimensional virtual entity.

Woman scrolled. Woman envied. Woman widow.

And you, the false widow, false, false.

A head on collision is inevitable by some design, grand or lowly.

In the wheelchair, hair unstyled, face unmade, wrapped in a camel tweed coat, is Mrs Higgs. You have not seen her in months, since you gave up the soft stalking, deciding some words should never be uttered, their atomic force never unleashed. There is very little of Charlotte Rampling left in her. The skin of her face is rice paper thin, eyes sunken like olive pits in the encroaching twilight as if she has not slept in nights. Apprehension anchors each movement.

'My keys, Vera, where are they? And my cards?'

'We left the cards at home, mother, and the keys are here. See?'

Vera strokes her mother-in-law's left shoulder and my god, how could you? How could you do it to this woman, this rose quartz of a woman. And how could he?

Vera smiles and in her face is a compelling guilelessness Instagram can't capture. She gazes down at Laura, cooing, 'What beautiful berries.'

Laura is Higgy and Hatzy, but in moments like these, you are glad her eyes are yours, dark and long-lashed. You don't think there is enough of him in Laura to alarm, the chin, the nose, yes, but in a sweeping, unstudied glance, she resembles you.

'I know you from somewhere.'

Mrs Higgs' sunken eyes are fixed upon you.

'Fabiana. The Italian restaurant.' Your response is immediate, your voice sounds borrowed. What is another lie on top of everything else? Is a lie worse when spoken in a graveyard than in a hotel room or supermarket?

'Yes, Fabiana . . . I remember. They make a nice lasagna there. We should come again. Vera, my credit cards, I can't seem to find them.' Mrs Higgs raises her white handbag towards her daughter-in-law.

Vera takes the bag, straps it over her then leans in and whispers to you, smelling of fresh shampoo, 'Don't mind mum-in-law. She's not much herself these days, or I guess, too much of her old self, like twenty-years-ago self.'

In another field, you might have been friends, good ones at that, but not in the Higgs field. The Higgs field won't allow it. Spin or sink.

You maintain a controlled, understanding expression, the one you've become adept at when a client is unsatisfied.

'Have you lost a parent? Or a husband? Is that why you've brought the child in here?'

Mrs Higgs' questions come rapid fire, uncharacteristic. But then, how would you know how uncharacteristic they are from perfunctory snippets in supermarket aisles?

111

'Oh, mother, we don't ask these personal questions.'

Here in this cemetery with its neat rows of skulls and spines and ribcages either side, you are the skeleton that has tumbled out, still in camouflage.

'I'm very sorry for your loss, whoever it may be,' Vera says and you are certain her atoms, her electrons, the fabric of her being must be iridescent, they cannot be of the same cheapness as yours, diamond to zirconium.

You need to condense your melting self and leave. Leave, leave before you become a pool of plasma between the graves.

Laura's head is pressing against your knee, but you don't want to lift her up just yet. You architecture a smile, a farewell.

'I can't seem to find my credit cards, Vera. Shall we call Peter at Deloitte?'

You walk faster towards the gates, hands fishing for the car keys in your handbag as Laura's head rests against your chin.

And when Laura drops the hypericum berries at the threshold of the cemetery, you stare at them in a radiation of horror. Only now, with the women deep in the cemetery does it dawn on you that the hypericum berries, in the vase of his grave, will be the extra particle, that added red-red mass, that will betray you in the Higgs field.

****

112

London Independent Story Prize 3rd Round Finalist

Sophia Skyers

TABLE FOR FOUR

A grainy image hangs to the left as you enter our dining room. A happiness observed. A perfect pose. Four chairs set around the mahogany table, a pendant light hovers, its circle of illumination reflects on the surface.

In the photograph, Royston, my father leans against the wall of a Victorian terrace. It's his sister's wedding. I rest against him; left arm around my shoulders, hand on mine to stop me squirming I imagine, in the way of four-year-olds. Oblivious to growing rancour. I appear insouciant, determined, Dad's little finger, bent outwards. 'Ouch Teresa' I imagine him saying. Cigarette in his right hand, lips parted, he stares ahead, sharp in black suit, waistcoat, white shirt, black bow tie, shiny black shoes. Though the picture is monochrome, memory supplies the colours: skinny walnut brown arms and legs stick out of my cornflower blue bridesmaid frock; my unruly hair, trained under a headdress.

Beatrice, my mother, stands to the left, nearest the camera. She arrived in Britain in 1954, the year before Dad. Their stars crossed in the canteen at the munitions factory. Mum is elegant, in a yellow dress, below the knee, close on the bodice, narrow on her slender waist, a crinoline flares the skirt. Joseph before her, hands in the air held by her fingertips, his tongue curling playfully towards his top lip. Nineteen months, he has a curated side part like Dad's, and in the fashion for boys, short blue trousers, a white short sleeved shirt, and blue bow tie. The bulge of his nappy shows. A moment in time, $1/200^{th}$ of a second.

We lived in Trenton Dale, a place seemingly unmoored, in the back-to-back terrace my parents bought in 1960, the year Joseph was born. The winter mornings brutal, stepping onto cold hard linoleum with bare feet. The drag, long and slow to market with Mum, the vacant cobbled streets, icy wind scraping my cheekbones. In the distance, naked silver birch limbs grazed the sky. Dad was a welder then. In the evenings I sat at the window in the front room, waiting for him to come home, the wan haze of a streetlamp visible through the nets. March 1964 segued into spring; My Boy Lollipop topped the hit parade. At family parties we danced together.

A new Rediffusion sat in the corner of our front room, opposite the window, its pregnant opal screen housed in a wooden cabinet stood on four stunted legs. In the afternoons, our favourite Watch With Mother played. Prancing Andy Pandy and Looby Loo; the staccato Wooden Tops, the garbled oddle poddle of Bill and Ben. When it finished, Mum turned the brown switch on the wall off. Joseph and I watched the white dot on the screen grow smaller and smaller and disappear. A make-believe safe space orbiting family, the shield from grim reality and calls to "go back to your country."

At home, our parents spoke Jamaican. Joseph, and I mimicked them. Mum would say, "Roy, stop massacre English." They spoke of "back home," "across the sea." Mum took us to the River Trent in the summertime. I imagined the sea to be like the river, people on the bankside smiling and waving, paddle boats bobbing, buoyed by gentle waves on a warm Autumnal afternoon.

An oak table was positioned in the back room, score marks, and place mats for our family decorating its surface. A ceramic teapot in a yellow knitted cosy on a mat, next to the toast rack. Mum bought our bread unwrapped, unsliced. "Naked bread" she called it. The centrepiece, an open fireplace and metal grate surrounded by beige tiles. A poker nonchalant on the right of the hearth. Dad's lighter and Woodbines occupied part of the mantlepiece nearest his armchair. When he came home from Fergus Welders, he sat, hunched in a swirl of acrid smoke, ball of his left foot on the hearth, Archers on the radio, accompanied by the fire's discordant splutter and gasp. I visualise Dad, white ash in his hair, eyes downcast.

Mum in her floral apron moved between the scullery and back room, setting the table, while dinner bubbled on the stove. She kept her Be-Ro recipe book in a cupboard above the wooden draining board, next to tins of beans, peas, corned beef, and rice. On the shelf below, on the right of the sink, the meat she bought every few days from Cyril the butcher, a box of eggs, potatoes, and onions. My upright piano inhabited the opposite side of the room, facing the fire. It gave off a musty odour when I opened the lid. To the right a door led to stairs and a dank cellar; a partial wall, exposed brick, and cobweb, divided the space. I sometimes held the torch going down to the cellar with Mum to fill the coal scuttle, or to put shillings in the meter. When I looked up towards the sliver of light from the chute, the ankles of people passing were visible. Mum took the tin bath from its hook in the backyard on Saturday nights for us to bath in the scullery. Monday, washday, she would "rub out the clothes" in the tin bath.

116

Winter on the cusp of spring 1968, my tenth year is when Toots and the Maytals' release, Do the Reggay. Desmond Decker's releases his Israelites later the same year, the first reggae number to reach the UK charts. I'm unaware of the malevolent cries, "Keep Britain White." My parents give me a watch on my tenth birthday. They come into the room I share with Joseph, across the creaking hallway from theirs. I'm in the military framed bed Dad got from his days in the RAF. Joseph in his single divan, near the sash window, claps. Dad leans towards me, secures the steel clasp on my birdlike wrist,

'You're double figures, and you will be as long as you live.'

'Not if I live to a hundred.'

'You might,' he says.

We camp in the Peak District, drive through pretty villages in Dad's Standard 10, wing mirrors like eyes on stalks. Chrome encases the oval grill in a broad grin, its nose the black and burgundy motor company crest. I bounce on the back seat, settle, elbow on the wheel arch; the odometer ticks over. Joseph's feet don't touch the floor. A family of four. Conspicuous. Children playing on a hostile landscape. Joseph and I ascend the hill at Thorpe Cloud. Mum and Dad skim stones across the Derwent; point out the ancient well dressing; we walk along the Tissington Trail. Dad makes tea on a camping stove; Mum chops stewing beef, potatoes, and carrots for dinner.

Saturday nights, we sometimes went to the Cavendish. The usherette's beam on the choc-ices on the tray before her. Joseph cried when the lights dimmed until Dad lifted him onto his knee, chin resting on the top of his head, lips brushing against his hair. Other Saturday's we watched television. The vaudeville Black and White Minstrel Show, white performers in blackface, made Mum and Dad angry. In the playground, we became targets of bullies, jostles, corrosive epithets, 'blackie' 'wog' nig-nog' 'sambo' 'sooty.' I squared up, fought back, returned punches, lost in a whirlpool of faces.

A month after my tenth birthday, Enoch Powell makes his Rivers of Blood speech in Birmingham, blames families like mine for Britain's economic woes. Dad says, 'He want us to go back to Jamaica. Even you two who born here.'

I recall my childhood naivety of people sailing to England on paddle boats, unaware my impression of the world was perceived through a prism of whiteness, a masquerade of neutrality.

Mum allows me to go to Valley Road Library alone, a short walk from home. On one visit, I choose the Famous Five, Rufty Tufty Runs Away, and Little Black Sambo. I go to return them in the afternoon. Joan the librarian looks at the stamp on my card, then at me. I like her because she's kind.

'You can't bring books back the same day.'

'I've finished them.'

'They are too easy for you. Ask Mum if I can come to see her.'

Later, a knock on the front door, I open it, Mum behind me, there's Joan. A trolley bus trundles by on the main road, its outstretched arm clutching the wire overhead emits a spark.

'I'm Joan Mason, the Librarian at Valley Road.'

118

'I'm Beatrice' Mum says, 'Come in.'

Joan climbs the three steps, enters the front room. Mum gestures towards the settee, they sit at opposite ends. I go to the armchair closest to Mum, my long legs dangle over the side. Joseph sits on the rug; arms encircle his knees drawn to his chest.

'Would you like tea?'

'Yes please.'

Mum goes into the scullery, returns with her best teapot on a tray, a jug of milk, a bowl of sugar, and two of her best China cups and saucers. They rattle when she places the tray on the coffee table. I spy custard creams on a side plate, sneak a peek at Joseph. He flashes a coy smile. Mum returns to the scullery; comes back with two glasses of orange squash she hands to Joseph and me. Mum sits on the settee, leans forward, pours the tea, offers biscuits to Joan; nods to Joseph and me to take one each.

'Your daughter's reads the books she chooses quickly.'

'She's always reading.'

Joan picks up her cup, blows on her tea, takes a sip, nods, and says,

'Would it be alright if I help her choose?'

'Yes of course.' Mum says. 'Thank you.'

I became absorbed in the lives of people from another time, and place, Oliver Twist, David Copperfield, Laura in Lark Rise to Candleford. I loved to read on my bed, a film of soot in the crevices of the sash windows where the glass met the wooden frame; the sun's glare muted by houses and belching chimneys opposite. I also read the scandalous Peyton Place. At my 50th birthday lunch as we mused on the past, Mum said playfully,

'Was I wrong to let you read it?'

'Yes.' I said. 'It was so risqué for a child.'

When I was around eight years old, Dad began to hold meetings in our back room with his white friends. In the front room watching television with Mum and Joseph, I heard their loud conversations. James, a friend of Dad's talked to Mum one day. He had fine blond hair; appeared tall, his tallness a childhood illusion. Mum leaned forward, polite, apparently engaged. James talked and talked. I absorbed random phrases, "revolution" "working class" "oppression." I ruminate now on Mum, enduring James' instruction. She came to Britain alone, from a former colony, familiarity behind her.

I play two-ball in the backyard against the scullery wall, Tosker three doors down barks. I sometimes toss a piece of slate from the roof onto numbered chalked squares and hop to retrieve it. Ghost tapping is a favourite game I play with my friends. We silently tie thread to a random door knocker, hide, pull the thread; tap-tap, tap-tap. It's hilarious, the confused face of whoever answers, and when realisation hits, an "Oi. Hop it." We earn pocket money carol singing. The first time, with my friend Patricia Riordan, we go to her house, rap on the door, begin. Her mother shouts,

'Ye sound like the cat's chorus. Be gone before I chuck a bucket of water over ye.'

She opens the door, laughing, hands us two shillings.

120

I discovered later, the pupils in my primary school came from places like Trenton Dale, places the Corporation saw as besieged. I began to understand the deceptive guises of bigotry from snippets of conversation between the older generation. Unaware of job insecurity at the time, I recall periods Dad was home to cook breakfast, and to take Joseph and me to school. Our extended family lived in walking distance. At one weekend gathering, I hear Dad say to his brother, Rupert,

'Everywhere them say "we don't employ your kind here."'

'One gal at my work ask if we live in trees where we come from.'

'I can't get a job. Bills have to pay; food have to buy.'

Years later Dad said,

'We heard about the colour bar back home. I thought it meant someone would say, "hi blackie" you would say, "hi whitey" and that would be it. I didn't know it meant you couldn't get a job or somewhere to live.'

'How did you manage?'

'It was easier then,' he said. "I went to night school and got government money to study full time.'

I'm age eleven, at the back of the class with my friends, a quintet, skylarking, squawking, crashing cymbals, a cacophony of anarchic sounds. Awkwardness invades the room when Mr Ashworth, calls me to the podium. My body tense, I walk to the front. He glowers, eyes condemning, tapping his wooden baton, rhythmically, a sadistic smile shackled to his face. His greasy hair, lank, in a basin cut, a flurry of dandruff on the collar of his black jacket. The silence stretches.

'Why are the troublemakers in this class all coloured?'

He points to me,

'You are. He is, she is, she is, and he is,' he says in the general direction of four black pupils. They stare ahead. Mr Ashworth turns to me again,

'How old are you?'

My face burns.

'I'm eleven sir.'

'Good. Any trouble and the courts can deal with you.'

At home, at the dining table, playing Ludo with Mum and Joseph, the threat lurks. I blurt out,

'Mr Ashworth says black children are bad.'

'What? I'll show him.' Dad, throws the Evening Post he is reading onto the rug, gets to his feet, comes close to me. A vein pulses at the side of his head. 'It's not true. Don't you worry'

When I was older, Dad told me he visited the headmaster and told him, "One more time and I'll take the lot of you to the Race Relations Board."

Life continued to circle around the everyday. The tooth fairy, Mum pressing my hair into teenage styles with an iron hot comb, clothes shopping with friends, listening to Alan Freeman's Pick of the Pops in my bedroom on Sunday nights. His "hello pop-pickers," three long rhythmical blasts, three staccato signature ones from the horns, another long blast, three staccato, and the characteristic melody.

In my third year of secondary school, my parents come in to talk about exams. I sit between Mum and Dad. A careers adviser faces us across an oblong Formica table. She studies her notes, raises her head, stares, and says,

'Hello, I'm Miss Walton. We have lots of pupils today, so I've got about twenty minutes.'

The classroom window ajar, the faraway drone of a lawnmower on the playing fields; the second hand on the wall mounted clock behind Miss Walton silently sweeps.

'Let's hope we can finish,' Dad says, 'we don't want you to be behind.' He adds, 'By the way, I'm Mr Royston Anderson, you can call me Roy, and this is my wife, Mrs Beatrice Anderson.'

The adviser purses her lips, focuses again on her notes, raises her head, fixes her gaze on Dad,

'Well, she's not exactly university material, is she?'

I gnaw my bottom lip. Mum stiffens in the chair to my right. I turn to Dad, his attention fixed on Miss Walton,

'You've been to university, have you?'

Without waiting for her reply

'My BSc is in Mathematics. Oh, and I teach in this city.'

I return my attention to Miss Walton, she reddens. I look again at Dad, eyes still fixed on Miss Walton, he smiles broadly,

'Our daughter can't decide whether to read Geography or Biology at university so, put her in for both subjects. Please.'

A photograph hangs in Mum's house, in the dining room, immediately opposite as you enter from the hallway. I study it now, off centre on the light blue wall, cocooned in a mahogany frame. A family. A perfect pose. Mum, black hair, grey streaks, stands to the left in a navy woollen blue jacket, matching skirt, white blouse. The middle finger and thumb of her right hand clasps the gold band on her ring finger. She beams at the camera. Next to her Joseph, grey suit, white collarless shirt, brown brogues, my Doctoral Tam perched on his head, lopsided, in a playful gesture, chicken pox scar above his left eye. Then me, three inches shorter than Joseph now, draped in a burgundy, black, and gold gown. My lips, parted, reveal the gap between my front teeth, a hallmark inherited from Dad. On the other side of me, Michael, my husband, slight build, studious in appearance, in a black suit, white shirt, and azure tie. In his arms, our three-year-old daughter Sasha has made a grab for his hair. The curb we stand below morphs into an expanse of grass and a distant ghostly silhouette of buildings.

The scent of rice and peas infused with coconut milk, garlic, and scallion, wafts into the dining room. It's accompanied by the clatter of crockery, Mum in the kitchen preparing to serve Sunday lunch. The faint hum of Bob Marley on the radio, No Woman No Cry; the chorus line, "Everything's gonna be alright, I say oh little darling, don't shed no tears." The early days and months were hardest. Now it's anniversaries, the small things; the way Dad drank tea, eyes closed, two sips in quick succession, a pause, eyes open. It's the fear of forgetting. I recall the final time I visited Dad in the hospice, his eyes occluded, skin jaundiced, a phantom, propped against a mound of pillows. I said to him, eyes full

'I'll live life for both of us.'

He replied, a low gravel, 'Do you fancy a game of scrabble?'

'No Dad,' I said. 'You always win.'

London Independent Story Prize 3rd Round Finalist

Joe Wedgbury

Where the Light had Once Been

For two years, we lived above the Palins; Anna and her husband Bob. Maggie called them The Palindromes.

In the mornings, Bob would leave for the job he didn't have in the car he didn't own and Anna would let the dogs out to piss. Maggie and I would stand on the balcony in the early pink haze, clouds thrown against the sky like bloody rags. We would drink coffee thick with grounds, and Maggie, in her tight-fitting holy jeans, would whisper, "How can he let her dress like that?"

Anna would sit on the low wall between the gardens and fuss at the dogs and rub her baby-belly and turn her back to us before lighting her cigarette.

"She must be awfully sad," Maggie would say.

It was late summer when Anna had begun to show; everything still held that touch of green. Maggie would wait for Bob to leave and she would take a bundle of knitting and a short stack of books and sit with Anna until the early evening.

"She's stuck for names for the baby," said Maggie, "so I'm helping her out. I thought of Elle and Hannah and Ava. It's trickier for a boy, but there's Otto, and I thought Nolon was nice. Nolon with an 'O'. Clever, don't you think?"

"She'll know what you're doing," I said.

Maggie smiled. "No, she's not too bright. Have you ever talked to her?"

"She makes passes at me when you're not around."

"You're almost funny."

"Who's joking?" I said.

Maggie pulled at the neck of her blouse and said, "I don't think I like Bob very much. I think he's cruel to her."

"Well, that's their lot," I said.

"We should have them for dinner," said Maggie, and that was that.

Maggie bought a whole side of salmon and she roasted it with lemon and rosemary and a tray full of fat Jersey Bennes. "Look at the colour on that," she said. "That's river-caught. Forget about that farmed stuff. See how red?"

"It's something," I said.

"Get the drinks," she said.

"Some whisky?"

"No, look; I'm making martinis. Get the white. And there's some grapefruit tonic for Anna."

Maggie took a bottle of gin and poured long measures into the mixer. She uncapped a new bottle of vermouth and spilled some into the cap and sipped at it. "Do you want a taste? It's kind of sweet."

"You're crazy," I said.

Maggie waved her hand. "See if we have olives," she said. "I want to make these dirty."

Maggie picked out some records and removed one from its sleeve and placed it on the turntable. She set the needle in the groove and danced as she crossed the room towards me.

"You're crazy," I said.

"I wish you'd stop saying that. Having fun isn't crazy. Enjoying yourself isn't crazy."

"You're the craziest thing I ever met."

We sat at the foldaway table in the kitchen and listened to the record and worked our way through the pitcher of martinis. Halfway through our third, Maggie started to soften. "I've got a little something else," she said. "We can smoke a bowl now, don't you think?"

"I thought you'd had it all?"

"I always keep a little something back," she said.

I looked at the clock above the refrigerator. "What time did you tell them?"

"Eight-thirty," she said. "Come on, they won't mind. Let's smoke a bowl."

The buzzer sounded and I went to the door. Anna was standing at the top of the stairs in her dressing gown. She looked pale and crooked and ham-faced and her eyes were yellow and wet.

"Tell Maggie I'm sorry," she said. "Bob's had to stay on at work."

"How are you, Anna?" I said.

"It's just the sickness. It went away and now it's back. And now I get these damn nosebleeds to boot."

"From the baby?" I said. "I never heard of that one."

"Well, what the hell would you know?"

"Why don't you come in for a while? You can sit with us until Bob gets home."

"No, I shouldn't. Tell Maggie I'm sorry. Tell her I won't be home tomorrow, but she can call in on Monday."

"I can send her down now, if you like?"

"No," said Anna.

"She's pretty dopey. You'd be doing me a favour."

"I have to say goodnight."

"Goodnight, Anna," I said.

Maggie was standing in the kitchen doorway. "What was that?"

"Said she's sick. Said Bob's working."

"Those lousy bastards," said Maggie.

"Ain't they just," I said. I took the whisky down from the top of the fridge and poured myself a glass.

"Working, my ass. What does she think, that I don't know?"

I shrugged and swallowed my drink.

"You know, I'm glad," said Maggie. "It'll be nice, just the two of us. We've got all this wine, and my beautiful fish. And you'll dance with me, won't you?"

"If I must."

"You don't have a trace of the romantic in you, do you?"

"I'm romantic."

"Oh, you used to be. I used to think I was damned lucky."

"Are you teasing?" I said. "I can't always tell."

"I am. I'm sorry. Sometimes I like a game."

We ate and drank the rest of the martinis and some wine, and Maggie fetched her little glass pipe and smoked the room up while I worked the bottle of whisky. The record on the turntable stopped and we heard voices carry up from downstairs.

"Do you hear that?" said Maggie.

"No," I said.

"That's Bob talking. Those lying bastards."

"What does it matter? This is better."

"Let's go down. Let's really let them have it."

"No." I got up and put another record on.

"He sounds angry, though, doesn't he?"

"That's their lot," I said.

I was brushing my teeth when Maggie came to the bedroom. She unbuttoned and removed her blouse and unhooked the side of her skirt and let it fall to the floor and climbed into bed. "Aren't you going to wash up first?" I said.

"I haven't the energy," she said.

"You're stoned."

She laughed brightly. "I'm really high. I went to the kitchen to do something and I couldn't figure out what it was. I stood there and I thought about it forever and the thought never came back to me."

"What about your medicine?"

"Oh, God damn it. Will you bring it to me?"

I opened the cabinet and found the clear bottle with the waxy yellow lotion. I took it to the bedroom and sat on the edge of the bed and shook Maggie's shoulder.

"Can't you do it for me?" she said.

"No," I said. "I'd get it wrong."

"I'd do it for you."

"I wouldn't ask."

"We have to take care of each other."

"I don't need taking care of."

"You will when you're older. When you're old and infirm I'll do all those things for you. I'll brush your hair and wipe your ass and dress you up in a special bonnet and parade you around the town."

"Here's hoping," I said.

Maggie groaned theatrically and righted herself on the bed. She took the bottle and she pressed the lotion onto her hand and smoothed it against the rough patches on her legs and arms and stomach. "I think it's getting better," she said. "There's a patch on my chest that only showed up yesterday, but everywhere else it looks like it's working." She stood up and went to the vanity dresser and turned about in front of it and angled the mirrors so that she could see all of her body. "Don't you think it looks good?"

I came and stood behind her and put my hands on her hips. "It does." I moved my hand from her hip to her breast and pushed myself in closer behind her.

She turned upwards, smiling, and she kissed me. "Do you want to?" she said.

"Always," I said.

"Okay!" she said. "Hold on." She gave a short wiggle and she pushed back from the vanity to move me away and she went to the bathroom. "You'll have to do the work," she said, "Boy, am I gone."

"Are you sure you want to?"

"You bet," she said. "I think I like stoned sex the best. Don't you? I left a little something in the kitchen, if you want to catch up with me?"

"I'm fine. We'll both be out of action."

"Screw you," she said, pulling off her underwear.

Afterwards, I lay on the bed and listened to Maggie run the tap and the water splashing as she washed her face and brushed her teeth. I heard her spit and hang up her toothbrush and I watched her step into the light of the bedroom.

"Jesus, the stink in here," she said. "Come out to the balcony with me."

We stood out on the balcony and Maggie smoked her cigarettes and we watched the lights from the low-hanging planes keel in towards the airport across the way. The sliding door sounded beneath us and we watched Anna come out to perch on her little wall. She sipped closely at a mug of something.

Maggie said, "So much for being sick."

"She's bringing the dogs out, see?"

"I've told her so many times, she mustn't keep smoking. Last week I hid her cigarettes."

The dogs fawned at Anna's lap and she ignored them. She took a short bottle from her dressing gown pocket and poured a thick schlock into her mug and took a deep swallow, and in the fuzzy half-light we saw her wince. She took another long drink straight from the bottle.

"That little brat is getting canned," said Maggie.

"You don't know that," I said.

131

"Oh, that bitch. That awful woman."

"Let it ride, will you?"

"The hell I will," said Maggie. "You saw it, same as I did." She leaned over the railing and called out, "Anna!"

Anna looked up slowly and brushed some of the hair from her eyes. She stared up at us and said nothing. I wasn't sure for the dark, but one of her cheeks looked stretched and puffy.

Maggie gripped the balcony rail so tight that I could see her knuckles quiver. "Anna! Don't you come to me for nothing!" she said.

The dogs relieved themselves and trotted inside. Anna stood up and ducked in behind them, a ragged little hound herself. Maggie was crying. She spat the filter from between her teeth and hissed, "Tangerine witch!"

It was hot that night and we lay above the covers. Maggie said, "That poor little baby. I can't stop thinking about it."

"It's like you said; she must be very sad."

"I think I hate her. God damn it, I do. I'd hate anyone who'd have it in them to do something like that."

"You don't hate her."

"Yes I do," she said. "Don't you see how unfair it is?"

I reached out and put my hand against her stomach and found my way down to the thick, rosy-pink scar beneath her navel. "You know we would have," I said. "If we'd got the timing right."

"You bastard," said Maggie. "Oh, you bastard. How can you say that to me, now?" She turned away and pulled the sheets around her. I reached out again and she pushed me away.

I moved to my side of the bed and shut off the lamp. The bulb in the hallway was flickering and sent spasms of light through the slip in the doorway. I closed my eyes and felt Maggie shaking from across the bed. Finally she said,

"That fucking light."

I rose and went out to the hall. I pressed the switch and I stared as the bulb cut out and the hot yellow filament faded. I stood there for the longest time, naked in the dark, watching the space where the light had once been.

Koushik Banerjea

Short Circuit

The curtailed pleasures of hard winter were starting to lift. Details she daren't divulge else her own brood might suddenly turn on her, arriving at certain conclusions; ones which left her at their mercy. The one place she really didn't want to be.

She dreaded the longer days for their enhanced social potential. The risk that one or other of her children, or of their children, several of whom were now also living on their own in this city, might drop by unannounced.

'Kaman aacho, Thamma?'

'Aachi. Kono rokom e cholchey,' she would dutifully reply, looking wearily at her grandson or granddaughter, and knowing full well her weariness was already being misread as wistfulness. Not that she blamed them though. It can't exactly have been reassuring for them to hear from their Thamma that she was 'somehow getting by.'

They were sweet enough really, and it wasn't that she didn't love them. She did, tremendously, just not when they would show up while she was watching the omnibus edition of *Neighbours*.

The longer days meant she no longer had a seasonal alibi for keeping the curtains drawn well before nightfall. Besides, that would only have further encouraged them. In their inchoate understanding, drawn curtains meant illness. Calls would be made and, lo and behold, it wouldn't be long before the entire clan was trooping through the door, all thinking they were 'performing their duty.'

And again, it wasn't that she didn't love her own children. She did, wholeheartedly, except for all those times they just wouldn't leave her in bloody peace.

After the death of her husband, God rest his soul, it was assumed by everyone that she would go and live with her eldest son, as was generally the custom. He had already made extensive renovations to his house, creating an extra bedroom with an en suite downstairs so that she wouldn't have to traipse up and down stairs every day on her crumbling joints. Her *Bouma* (daughter-in-law) was already making plans, plans, so many plans for her, and she hadn't even agreed to move in with them.

Where they would go and what they would do.

Aamra eykhaney jaabo aar eta korbo.

Or on another day a list of galleries, museums and restaurants they would be visiting. This place and that place and this painting and that statue. But she said it all a little too quickly, too easily. As though it was a weight, an unwelcome duty she had been carrying this whole time and couldn't wait to unburden herself of.

Duty.

What a strange idea. In her experience, not so much when it was applied to marriage (she'd expected, they both had, to honour certain 'duties'), but rather to all those elements which came afterwards.

Family. Appearance. Expectation. That last one especially.

She knew her family talked about her when she wasn't there, and could easily imagine the form those conversations might take.

Why is she so stubborn? She can barely cope. Why is she making this so hard for everybody?

Her eldest son's face slowly growing into his father's, but with none of the trademark humour. For it was true, Vishal was always so serious, whether he was project managing home improvements or meeting with his financial advisor to discuss ongoing and future investments. And his eager, eager wife, with an opinion on so much, including all the things she clearly knew so little about. Books, culture, sport, politics, all of it fair game to a mind evidently unburdened from older notions of duty. Or decorum. And weren't those things just as important as expectation and appearance? But she knew her brood well enough not to press the point. They loved her and in the end they meant well. Yet while the arthritis attacked her joints and the osteoporosis took its toll on her bones, she couldn't shake the feeling that it was actually her children who were the brittle ones. So easily offended, but unsure what to do with those feelings. And, in a way, she was grateful for that too. *They* had never seen cutlass slice through bone, never felt terror under tarpaulin at a roadblock, never smelt death coming from the jute mills. So quick to anger but so without shame too. Joking and laughing with one another but then all of a sudden serious when looking at her. As if she was somehow intruding upon *their* happiness. And yet when she made it clear that she would be staying in her own home, that she had no intention of moving in with any of her children, their expressions would change again. This time, a note of disappointment to go with the consternation. And in the telling detail about 'convenience,' and how she wouldn't even have to go up and down stairs anymore, what she actually sensed was just how *inconvenient* her 'needs' were becoming, if not for her then certainly for her children, to whom she had never wanted to be a burden.

'But Ma, all the renovations are done. Everything you need is downstairs. Upureh aar jettey hobey na. Khub shubida hobey.'

'Ha, aami shob shunlam, kintu amar nijjey bari te thakbo. Eta shobchey shubida hobey.'

And it was true, she had no intention of leaving the home she had lived in for forty years, where she and her husband had raised their family to *not* know the corrosive effects of upheaval, of homelessness, of sharing the night sky with neighbourhood strays. She caught her Bouma looking at her then, if only momentarily, with something close to hatred. For a split second was all it took to see beyond the façade. Plans tumbling away to leave just an empty interior with too many bathrooms.

Her daughters too had offered many times to have her move in with them. But this idea appealed even less. It cut against the grain of every custom she had ever been raised with. And of course she knew the arguments against this, the ones put forcefully enough by her daughters themselves and sometimes even by their husbands, though she had difficulty believing them. It was hard to trust the opinion of people who were so rooted in the here and now that they seemed to have forgotten her longer lifespan. A 'there' and a 'then' always in play too.

How would they have coped? Not well, she fancied.

Mosquitoes, kerosene lamps, no stove. And what about the noise, or the heat, or the uncertainty, one day from the next, as to who might be on the other side of the door? Nightfall a shroud of heightened anxiety. The worst times punctuated by the howl of the mob, of running and shouting and screams. The smell of burning, the whole of *then* aflame.

Her daughters, Sharmila and Amrita, who had barely ever brought her so much as a cup of tea when they had still been living under her roof. And now *they* were going to look after her in her dotage?! The very thought was absurd. Amrita, the younger of the two, did at least have the good grace not to pretend it was a good idea.

'Why don't you move in with us?' she asked, utterly without enthusiasm, and only after all the other options on the table appeared to have been exhausted.

They were sat in Vishal's living room, which for some reason he insisted on calling a lounge. Only in her head, full of 'then,' was it still a bosharghar, but these days even sitting was an effort, and her legs were raised on a footstool.

All four of her children and their partners were there, as well as her oldest grandson and his 'friend,' who everyone seemed to know was his girlfriend. Not everything about now was bad, she reflected. At least some of that dhak dhak business of the past was lifting, and that was a good thing. The girl too seemed nice enough. In fact it was she who had brought over the footstool from another room and then very tenderly made sure that Thamma's legs were also cushioned on the stool. She was pretty as well. Freckles and kind eyes and the beautiful, ocean curled hair of Kerala. Later, she learned from her grandson that the oceans in question were in fact the Caribbean and Irish seas, and the name on their lips was Siobhan.

Her Bouma, whom she refused to call by any other name, had had the evening 'catered.' Eleven of them in total and she had brought caterers in. Her late husband would have found it amusing, the mere concept of caterers, though in truth she herself wouldn't have objected. After all, it was never her husband who had had to rise with the dawn chorus to start preparing the extravagant spread, which every guest had come to expect from one of their gatherings. Several tarkaris, dal, maach, mangsho, raita, ruti, special fried rice as well as pulao, sandesh, mishti doi, all reliant on labour intensive dicing, rolling, stirring, chopping. Then frying, boiling, straining, blending. Marinades, mustard seeds, maddening Bengali detail. No, she wouldn't have minded caterers on those occasions, but the thought had never even occurred.

Her husband was still working in the factory then, that wretched building that would eventually doom him with its thankless piece work and asbestos lining. But they hadn't known at the time, and were grateful for the money, which in any case was stretched very thin once the remittance to the family back 'home' was deducted from the ironically termed 'take home pay.' Whose home? she regularly wondered, as she found herself at yet another jumble sale, picking out a luckier family's castoffs for her own restless brood. Her cheeks flushed with shame every time she was forced into this economy, but she consoled herself with the knowledge that they did at least live in their

139

own home, and so were not at the mercy of 'the Corporation,' or as it was known here, 'the Council.' Secondhand clothes were a small price to pay for peace of mind. A key turning a lock and then escape within, everything else left at the front door with the shoes.

Prashant, the younger of her two boys, was sat opposite her, nimbly eating with his fingers. Around this table he was the only one of her children to do so, deftly ensuring that no food left a passable trace above the first phalange. Her husband would have approved, God rest his soul. And he would surely have enjoyed watching Prashant's 'friend,' David, who everyone seemed to know was his boyfriend, carefully mimic the subtleties required to avoid the sloppy brutishness of higher phalanges besmirched by food. However, there was never any question of her going to live with them. Zone 1, no decent nearby food markets, and worst of the lot, a loft conversion with few soft edges but a whole lot of hardwood flooring. She didn't begrudge him any of it though. Like all her children, he had worked hard to build a successful career for himself. Why shouldn't he also enjoy the trappings? It was a long way from jumble sale chic, and further still from her own origin myth.

A professor's daughter, a Brahmin, loved and respected and wanting for nothing. And then almost overnight, a refugee, an outcast, haunted by what she had seen and heard, and lucky to escape with even the clothes on her back. Then still a young man, her future husband had also narrowly avoided the sectarian frenzy of that time, of cutlass on bone, though it would be many years later before their eyes first found one another across a crowded factory canteen. And that too in a very different city, of fog and smog and the nauseous smell of lard every dinner time. He'd eaten with his fingers that first day. She still remembered, it was a cheese and pickle sandwich, and she had been impressed by how little the acrid tang of the pickle seemed to bother him. 'It's local achar,' he had told her across the formica top, eyes glinting with imported mischief. After that the canteen was where they would meet, and where she would tell him about her family, the ones left behind and the ones who never made it. She in turn would hear of his ancestral village and the horror which engulfed it when the mob arrived, eyes already aflame from some incendiary speech or lethal rumour. He described the tarpaulin under cover of which a kind stranger had smuggled him across the new-fangled border, and she told him about the constant struggle to keep her one sari and blouse clean while all around her the bodies, the heat and the dust kept mounting. And then without warning one day she found herself eating the pickle without grimacing, and just like that the stories dried up. Or rather *those* stories ended, quickly displaced by newer ones, about buses and pea soupers and punch cards and unhygienic cooking fat. A here and a now in which the Brahminical stipulations no longer seemed to matter so much. Who you ate with, who you worked with, even who you slept with. All of it sloughed off, like a dead skin. The moulting largely irresistible, as if they had both just been waiting, all along, for the first available opportunity to start afresh. And in this knowledge they felt so giddily light, so enraptured, that they forgot to nurse resentment each time an unkind look, or a curse, or a hawked saucer of phlegm came their way from one of the locals.

No Council house, no problem; no mortgage, no problem; no credit of any kind, no problem; no love in the eyes of the not-so-fresh-fruit seller, no problem; no water in the municipal baths with which to wash that beautiful Indian hair, no problem.

Instead, the unspoken grievances found succour in saving up little by little and out of sight, until first a tiny flat, then a maisonette, then finally a dilapidated house in one of the city's most rundown districts could be called home. And *this* was the home in which she had raised her family, and in which she still lived and fully intended to stay.

Her Bouma must have gone to great lengths to find caterers who supplied dishes which were so close, in texture and flavour, to her own, and the thought briefly lingered that she was being reminded of her own obsolescence in such matters. The caterers absorbed every demand, and the pressure those came with, that she had once done. And all this just so her Bouma wouldn't have to, leaving her or more likely Vishal free to broach the subject her family had clearly been gathered here to discuss.

'So, Ma, have you thought about what we spoke about last time?' asked Vishal, casting his wife a quick, sideways look.

'Aami ki abar bolbo? Aar aamar koto baar eki jinish boltey hobey? You stay happily in your house, aar kono rokom e I stay in mine. Eta shob deeg thik e bhaloey hobey.'

'But everything is ready for you here, Ma. Tomar aar ranna ghar e jettey hobey na. Aajkal baire thik e shob powah jai. Anything you want, any special food, anything really, we can get for you. And no need to worry any more about shopping, or bills, or those fence panels that keep collapsing.'

Her husband, God rest his soul, had always been the one to carry out any domestic repairs, and for as long as he was alive they had barely ever needed the services of a plumber, or electrician, and most certainly not those of a gardener. Under his magic touch, aloo, mint, grapes, even pumpkins, had flourished, as though he were still the country boy with planting, growing, nurturing in his fingers. A folklore never fully worn down by the tincture of arc welders, grinders, or lathes on nightshifts. And most certainly the equal to any minor repairs. They might not have raised their children in the old ways, but that didn't mean letting go of everything. For the past could still be seen in the deft manipulation of soil, or of pipework, or circuitry, which sprang from harder times and hotter climes. Ingenuity was also the key in her small kitchen, where unpromising raw materials would magically be transformed into renowned feasts. And yes, caterers might have been welcome, but that word didn't yet exist for their circumstances. It belonged to a different breed, one which over time her children evidently felt some affinity for. She looked around the table and saw the eager, expectant faces hungry for her submission, which of course she knew from her doctor was nowadays called 'consent.'

Siobhan and her grandson gave her a lift home and gently chaperoned her inside, waiting until she was safely propped up in her favourite chair before making their excuses. The dinner had broken up quickly after her refusal to concede, but she had stayed long enough to overhear her Bouma and Vishal arguing in the study. It was difficult to make out exactly what was being said, but the words 'expense' and 'ungrateful' kept being repeated, each time with seemingly more local achar, and its original, acrid tang, in the delivery. You didn't escape the past, she thought, but if you were lucky it sometimes let you go.

       Playing with the television remote control, she chanced upon a familiar scene. *Neighbours'* Ramsay Street, bathed in regulation optimism, after a scheduling blip which meant its usual early evening timeslot had been usurped by a special documentary to mark the passing, several days previously, of some important politician. The picture quality was briefly marred by interference and she found herself furiously pressing the buttons on the remote, but to no avail. Then to her immense relief a message came up on the screen apologising for the interference and reassuring viewers that normal service would soon be resumed.

London Independent Story Prize 3rd Round Finalist

Perdita Stott

Salt

We're going to play a game, one where we pretend you are not dying and I still love you.

The human head is heavier than you would expect. You might think it's weighed with thought, but it's the liquid. And the bone. Bone and water, the heaviest of all living things and all living things, came first, from the water. Living calcium. Brain waves.

The thunk, as your head hits the hardwood floor, makes me think of conkers. Autumn chill in the air, polished shiny surface. Harder to crack than expected.

You're due your medication in half an hour. Do I still try to give it to you? Pry your lips open and force them in one by one. Wrapped in peanut butter or cheese, the way we used to disguise pills for the dog so she would stop throwing up in the Volvo every time we went to the beach.

I miss the sea. The unmarked map of its horizon. The clanging ghost story of its depths. It is our first home, tiny microcosms, splitting cells till we can crawl out onto the land to become reptiles to become beasts to become monkey creatures who still grow our babies in water. Waters break and life begins. If I mend your waters, will your life end?

Your hand is cold in my sweaty palm, like holding a limp leather glove as if there's nothing really in there. It makes your lips twitch in the ghost of a smile though, so I keep it there. Love is a knife. If I hated you, this would be easy. If I had never loved you, this would be sad. What is it now? What are we now?

Getting you to the car is the hardest bit. I have to go down backwards, timid toe testing the step behind me, my arms jammed under yours as your feet drag and dangle on the top step. I didn't put your shoes on, there didn't seem any point, but now the sight of your naked toes makes me feel guilty. I think of your childhood toes buried in the sand as they must have done years before I knew you. Our feet are free as children. It's only grown-ups who like to trap them in shoes, buying more than we need in different styles. Pretty prisons. I vow to myself that if I ever have a child, I will never force it to wear shoes. Although the chances of that now seem slim.

I drive with the windows down, the way we did when we were younger, the way we did before you got sick. You feel the cold too much to enjoy it these days, but it doesn't matter now. You're laid out on the back seat, like a rolled-up carpet, your pale feet pressed up against the glass of the window. I roll it down slightly so the baby pink face of your big toe can peep out. Your mouth does another upward twitch, so I leave it like that.

The dog used to travel with her head out the window. Soft black ears streaming and pink tongue lolling.

"There's a special joy in watching a dog be so happy." You would say, one hand on the steering wheel, the other leaning

146

casually out the window. You drove the way I imagined James Dean drove.

The dog is what I miss the most. It broke my heart to give her away and I couldn't even bring myself to be happy for the family who adopted her. I could only hate them and hate you, for making me choose.

"It's going to be too much to cope with," my mother told me. "You can't take care of him and the dog. It's not fair to any of you. Especially the dog. "

That was the bit that got me, how she persuaded me. She always knew how to guilt me into action.

It wasn't too bad for a while. You were brave, and I was caring. We damned up the cracks in our relationship with this new drama, hoping it would be big enough to make the smaller dramas seem irrelevant. The Godzilla of cancer would bring us closer together. We would rise to the occasion, our big movie-ending moment. But all we knew was how to drown. Even as we clung to each other, calling it commitment, we were only dragging each other down.

You are not allowed to resent dying people, which only made me resent you more, and all the things that irritated you about me became magnified. Burst into technicolour. Like Dorothy stepping into Oz, our world bloomed into full-colour dissatisfaction.

You couldn't leave because you were already on your way out, and I couldn't leave because it would make everyone uncomfortable to watch their friend leave their dying husband.

I wonder sometimes what would have happened if I had left before you knew you were sick or, better yet, if you had walked out on me, maybe a year ago, before you noticed the symptoms. We would live our lives, oblivious, or at least I would. Then, I would hear what had happened, at a dinner party or maybe through a mutual friend. I would feel genuine sympathy. I would rush to your side and you would pretend like you didn't need me.

"No, no, I'm not your problem anymore," you would say, noble and handsome. Not yet in your sickbed.

But I would insist. I could be tender, shedding a single movie star tear as I caressed your forehead. You would like how that felt, and I could still look at you.

You'd have a nurse, of course, but I would visit every day, with flowers and books and fond nostalgia for our time together. I would be a visitor, not a prisoner. I could go home at the end of each day and sleep through the night without having to wake in fits of fear in case you stopped breathing.

Or maybe I wouldn't find out until the very end. Then I would arrive, dressed elegantly in black with photographs and fond memories.

Maybe that would have been for the best. You wouldn't have to be exasperated by me and I wouldn't have to resent you.

I keep the window rolled down the entire way and speed up. You always liked to go fast. I can almost see the blue horizon of the sea.

We met in the sea, a long-ago holiday, when we were both young enough to believe we could be anything we wanted. Before we knew what we wanted. Two separate friendship groups, the girls and the boys. A trip to Crete, pretending not to notice each other as we splashed in the bath warm blue of the Mediterranean sea. I wasn't a strong swimmer, so when I felt hands grip my ankles and drag me under, I thought I was going to die. My cry of shock did nothing but fill my mouth and nose with water as a rush of bubbles flew past my eyes, and my ears filled with the clanging of deep water. I thought I had been taken by a vengeful sea creature or merman searching for a drowned bride. And then your smiling face appeared, laughing underwater with seaweed black hair floating around your face. You kissed me once and then, strong arms guiding me up, helped me to the surface. I was so shocked by the kiss (my first) and so relieved to be breathing again that I couldn't help but think of you as my saviour. Conveniently forgetting that you were the one who had pulled me down in the first place.

The sea was always our place, our special spot. You once told me you wanted to be buried at sea.

By now, the hospice nurse will have arrived at the flat and realised that we are gone. I didn't bother to lock the front door. She increased your pain medication last week, warning that it might inhibit your speech. We didn't bother telling her you hardly speak to me these days, anyway. I tried to feel bad about the amount of pain you must be in for you to ask for more pills. You always hated taking pills. But every four hours I would hold them out and you, baby bird mouth gaping, would accept them. The trapdoor hinge of your jaw exhausted you, so I would leave you alone for another four hours. And another and another. Again and again, never missing a dose, even the midnight waking ones.

I was dutiful, you were docile. You were always good at working two angles.

It is still early enough for the beach to be deserted. A couple of dog walkers are dots in the distance, and seagulls cry above our heads. I can taste salt on my lips. At first, I thought it was the sea air until I realised I'd been worrying my lower lip so much that I'd cut it and my mouth was tasting blood. And I think about how water and blood taste of salt, of the ocean. Where all life comes from. The air has the whisper of rain on it and a chill breeze comes off the grey water. I think I prefer the beach like this, more than when it's sunny. I think about how we used to pack sandwiches and flasks of tea and sit in the car, our bare feet wedged up on the dashboard as we watched the waves surge closer and closer up the sand. How we would run out, cackling in the rain, to dance and kick sand and kiss under a steel sky. When I think about the last time we ever did that, my memories, though sweet, have become muddled. I sit for a while, not taking my hands off the steering wheel, and listen to the sound of the waves and the erratic rattle of your breath. I half expected you to stop breathing on the way here. I half wanted you to, but now I'm glad that we have both made it. I sit and watch the warmth of our breath slowly steam the windows. It's been more than a week since I last heard your voice. I wonder what you would say to me now.

There is a species of sea slug that steals the venom of other creatures. It collects the stingers from more deadly fish, able to creep close, despite its soft body. In fact, it's because of its softness that it's able to deflect the poisonous spines. It collects them and hoards them until it needs them.

I wonder if people will say I should have been watching you more closely if maybe I did this to you. Maybe that's what you wanted them to think. I'm not sure how long you've been saving your painkillers, maybe ever since they upped your dose. I should have been checking your mouth, forcing it open after each swallow the way they do in movies. I think about you tucking the pills into the secret soft skin of your cheeks so you could spit them out later.

It must have tasted awful.

How did you decide that today was the day? You must have grown too weak before you could swallow them all. The little white pellets scattered across the bedspread, like a message to me. I probably wouldn't have noticed anything if you had taken them all.

It took me a minute to realise what they were. It looked as if you had spilled salt or something. Scattered breadcrumbs to find your way back home through the forest. How did you know when you'd had enough?

Your breath, like torn silk, is rattling but regular. Your eyes are shut, but when I twist around in the driver's seat to whisper, "We're here," I'm certain I see another one of those half twitches, a ghost smile, on your face. I know you've had enough. We both have.

I thought it would be harder to get you to the water, but there's nothing much left of you and I have grown strong lifting you to the bathroom and back to the bed. My mother used to warn me about getting too muscular in the arms.

"Men don't like that."

"Do you mean men like women to look weak?"

"It's just not very feminine looking. Don't pull that face. I only say these things to help."

The funny thing was, everyone said what a strong woman my mother was. They came up to me all day at the funeral to tell me.

"She was so strong."

"The strength it must have taken to raise you, alone."

"She was a tough old bird."

I realised then what she had meant, that I needed to look weak but always, secretly, be stronger.

I lie you down on the plastic sheet I brought with us and drag you across the sand to the edge of the waves. I take off my shoes and socks, feeling the wet sand bulge between my toes. It looks almost black in the overcast light, cool against my bare feet. When I step into the water, I gasp from the cold but keep moving, dragging you behind me. The water reaches my knees and then my waist. It's easier to move you, the further into the waves we go. I push you out in front of me, like a surfboard, bobbing through the grey water. I'm standing on my very tippy toes now, the water lapping at my chin and filling my mouth with salt water. The sand beneath me, I know, is going to suddenly drop. It catches swimmers out every year. People drown here. I think about the first time we met. You almost shut your eyes, and as you float on your back, I can see a small opening at the very edge of your eye - can you see the sky? My toes are straining now, balancing like a ballerina. I have to let go or fall. I push myself up and out of the water and when I come back down, my mouth is on yours, my kiss pushing us both down beneath the waves.

London Independent Story Prize 3ʳᵈ Round Finalist

Helen Kennedy

Malakai Can't See the Moon

The milking mothers sit in Victoria Park in a fairy circle, making windmill arms. They clap and sing, pirouetting their puppet babies to the music. She supports Malakai, keeps him upright, even though he'd like to flop. His eyes rolling around. The mothers share a knowing look, and she feels a stab of hurt. She lies Malakai on the yoga mat. He is motionless, as the other babies kick and raise their heads like sphinxes. Afterwards, she listens to the mothers talk about muscle tone and cranial massage, kombucha shots and the benefits of Senegalese cotton. She pushes Malakai's arms into coat sleeves and waits until the mothers have stepped away, folding their babies into tech pod prams. The Baby Sharks lady says a half-hearted well done.

She walks home the long way, circling Regent's Canal, drowsy and dank with residual rain. The weather slants across the horizon. There are days when she makes three circuits to get Malakai to sleep, alongside the skateboarders and runners, the Tai Chi silhouettes of women and the oul fellas on park benches waiting to unravel their sleeping bags. The sweet smell of the beat box boys smoking weed in the Chinese Pagoda. Bethnal Green is grey and glassy, the long line of graffitied shop windows pixelated with rain. Roman Road is narrowed with buses. Behind the old Council offices are concrete high rises, high rent flats with narrow stairwells and landings crowded with pushchairs and bikes. It's an anonymous place. Outside, Mr

154

Benjamin is planting containers of stringy green beans and firecracker chillies in the rain, his head buried in his coat. He lives up on the third floor and she hears him haul compost up and down, dragging it past her front door and leaving soil everywhere. She carries the buggy up two flights of steps, the lift they call 'the coffin' is broken again.

She gives Christopher in the next door flat a wave through the gauzy curtain and imagines him waving back. On the other side of the door, he is breathing heavily. She turns the key quietly to not wake the baby. Through the thin wall, the sound of Christopher's taps, washing and rewashing his hands, the water rushing down drains and gurgling through pipes. Sloughing off skin and dirt trapped in between walls and in cracks in the ceiling. She leaves his double-bagged Iceland shopping on the landing. Christopher will decontaminate it in the middle of the night, store it with the hundreds of plastic bags piled up for a nuclear winter. He has told her that she and Malakai will be the lucky ones when the day comes. He's got plenty of canned food, and follow-on milk, even nappies and wipes.

In the flat, she opens the window, stands, and stares at the melancholy skies. It is only then that she can breathe. Forcing the feeling out that has tightened around her chest. Developmental milestones missed, the health visitor who can't tick her tick boxes. Malakai wakes and she releases him to stretch on the floor like a lean cat. She heats a bottle of baby milk and sits by the window watching the rain fall. At eye level, she watches couples in neighbouring flats through kitchen windows, dogs tied up on balconies, a man masturbating infront of the TV. The east end urban landscape. Below the hum of electric buses, throaty motorbikes, and braking cars. Malakai sucks lazily on the teat, the rise and fall of his chest like elastic. When he is in her arms like this, orbiting each other, nothing else matters.

155

When Malakai was born, he breathed mechanically through tubes, was fed by a pump and a syringe driver. His pale blue eyelids shut tight. The incessant call of alarms and nurses in blue scrubs. The long nights in amber lit stairwells, smoking. She whispered to him to hold on, and that's what he did, near to death. Sometimes she dreams it didn't happen. When Malakai is asleep, he is whole and perfect, and no one can tell her otherwise. Down in the community space, Mr Benjamin is planting up oil drums with red chard and squashes, bok choi and green beans. The soil dark and heavy with rain.

The next day the health visitor is at the front door, waving her hands and lapping up Malakai like a puppy. Its all about recording, weight, length, the circumference of his head. Things on the outside. What about his brain? she wants to say. Malakai can't see the moon. At the front door, the health visitor touches her arm. 'Let's see how he's doing next week,' she says, a gentle reminder that she is a mother being watched, monitored.

Sometimes she dreams of Cal, he had been there and then he had not. He was a man who sang about a future but couldn't seem to find it with her, strumming a guitar and making her feel loose. She had loved him then, in her bed and lying under the canopy of broad-leaved trees in the park, that long summer when he hung around. Their voices drifting through hazy afternoons, and dreamy nights. London was lazy with heat, beer- can laughter in the street, the heavy smell of spice and burning barbecues. Sometimes we don't see love leaving until its already gone. She hasn't heard from Cal in over a year. Word is that he's touring round Europe, that he will be back in the Autumn, but she can't rely on the unreliable.

She watches Malakai sleeping, open mouthed. The sweep of dark dusted eye lashes and his sweet milky breath. He has the same smooth skin as Cal. Long limbs. In these moments, the world seems the right way round.

Mr Benjamin is out in the squally wind with a spade, putting black compost into old tyres. He kneels down like he's praying, and carefully makes circles of green seedlings. He sees her watching and gives her a wave. Next door, Christopher's curtains are closed, the duct tape around the windows and letter box, sealed inside. The flickering streetlights are a sign of ionising radiation from outer space, he once told her. They can fry your insides. She checks her watch. Its after midday, and she listens at the door. The sound of violence, the ack-ack of video games on the other side. She leaves rice and peas, fried chicken, (no spice because it's infrared) double wrapped in clingfilm.

Bethnal Green is becoming bourgeoise, mummies with designer pushchairs stand in line outside the Young V&A, talking in cut glass accents. The Buddhist centre has opened a vegan café, young techies at glass tables and sunny yellow paintwork. A small courtyard hung with tassels and wind chimes. At the charity shop, she buys babygros, socks and hand knitted cardigans. The woman behind the counter reaches out to touch Malakai's small fingers and smiles. He's a proper peach, she says. Outside, the Deliveroo bikers stand in a cloud of cigarette smoke, orange padded bags strewn across the pavement. London streets are flytipped, alive with hip hop bagel shops and greengrocers taking up box space on the pavements. Mobile phone shops flashing neon. On the market, Assad in his Arsenal shirt, sells vapes and knock- off Bulgarian cigarettes and tips her a wink. Outside the laundromat, Sherilee in her yellow and black headscarf, props the door open with her foot and screams has anyone got pound coins. Sherilee dances around with

Malakai in her arms as she does her weekly wash. The universe feels full of love.

At home, she makes purée, soft carrot, rice porridge and sweet potatoes. Every swallow is a milestone. She turns up Heart radio, dances to Raye. Christopher is listening through the thin walls. She makes sure he hears her sing. The low sun glances over the windowsill and heartened by it, she carries the pushchair down the steps. Mr Benjamin smiles up to his eyes when he sees her, pushes the cap back on the top of his head. His greying hair, jet dark eyes and skin. "He' bonny alright,' he says, jiggling Malakai's foot. She watches him plant up the containers. Fire-hot chillies and courgettes, Grobags with the earthy smell of tomatoes. A purple lilac bush breathes perfume. Mr Benjamin pulls up a rattan chair, lets her sit beside him. Malakai is wide eyed, following the shake and ripple of the fat green leaves. The waving of tree branches in the breeze. She closes her eyes and feels calm for the first time.

They watch the sky sink into molten layers above the city, orange, and gold. The warm wind feels restorative. Mr Benjamin pulls out a flask of dark rum and pours some into a plastic cup. It smacks her throat, hot and sweet like summer. Christopher is standing in the window, staring at the sunset. She waves and she likes to think that he gives her a thumbs up. Later that night, she will call an ambulance when the bath overflows out of the front door and two men in green uniform will bump him down the stairs strapped to a seat. Christopher barely conscious, and bandaged. The door to his flat left open. She will navigate the floor to ceiling emergency food rations and video games, to mop the bathroom floor and wipes the surfaces of blood.

That night she remembers Malakai's slow-motion birth, anaesthetised with gas, air, and anxiety. She pressed the alarm button on repeat, but it was three hours before they decided to release his stuck shoulder. Oxygen deficient written on the doctor's face. Malakai was breathless, blue, unresponsive. His see through skin and slack veins. Hospital hours were hateful, hushed into tight lipped silence. She waited. Hours and days of waiting when the world stopped turning. 'Incidental birth' was written in red pen on the medical notes.

August is exhausted. The city is thirsty and waits for rain. She helps Mr Benjamin haul buckets of collected water from the galvanised trough. The air smells like the sun. Malakai puts pea pods in his mouth and holds glinted cherry tomatoes in his small hands. Small things matter, the way he points at bees and makes their buzz sound. The golden sunlight catching his hair. Mr Benjamin holds Malakai as she picks feathery topped carrots and sweet raspberries, and everything feels possible.

One night, Cal knocks at the door, tanned and lean with a guitar slung over his shoulder. His smile and the heat make her lose her mind to him. He's been playing gigs, he says, made good money and the next morning he leaves it on the kitchen table. The smell of his strong pee in the unflushed toilet and her shame. She promises herself it's the last time, but she knows she's not good at promises.

Christopher comes home from hospital, and she cooks salt fish and vegetables, crumble and custard and leaves them in a sealed Tupperware box on the doorstep. His slow chime voice says, 'Thank you, Alisha.' Sometimes we can't navigate the solar system, and we have to start with a single day. In the middle of the night, she wakes to the sound of the rattan chair being moved outside Christopher's front door and listens to him singing soul.

She watches Mr Benjamin pick the last of the sweet peas, and ruby red chard. When she prises Malakai's fingers around the trowel, he screams with delight. Mr Benjamin holds him whilst she digs and sets the winter vegetables. 'Watch them grow,' he says.

London Independent Story Prize 3rd Round Finalist

Charlie Kite

We'll pay and we'll go

"It's far too expensive," Etta says again, cradling her handbag on her lap. She already knows she will not pay for dinner, but she has to pretend, do the dance.

"It's your present," Dani counters precisely. The worst part of it all, of course, is Etta knows that Dani knows that Dani will pay and Etta will not. It feels absurd. She shifts in her seat again, tugging at the skirt that really is too short for somewhere like this. Her neck feels itchy.

The whole thing had been totally middling. Dani had been going on about the restaurant for weeks, having been previously with colleagues. It was inevitable this is where Etta would spend her birthday. The food was fine, excellent of course but in a way that somehow becomes totally forgettable. Fine dining is often just fine. Etta came up with that forever ago and has been desperately trying to find an excuse to say it out loud to someone. Tonight is not the night, of course. Do the dance, do the dance.

"It was *so* good."

"Told you. Best bit?"

"Oh, the banoffee. You never get banoffee pie anywhere. Even deconstructed."

Dani smiles, that smug smile that is both irritating and sexy. Etta worries this describes Dani overall.

"I thought the starter thing, the scallops, they were great. Really nice jus."

"Yes, yes."

She picks at the dry skin around her cuticles and looks vaguely around for the waiter to reappear with the bill. God, it is a miserable place. The walls are covered with this grey, felty sort of fluff, interspersed with canvases of block colour, and the low amber light makes everything feel heavy and damp-seeming. Too quiet, too, a good number of empty tables. It is a random Wednesday, she supposes, but still, fancy place like this, you would expect more. It makes everything awkward, as if having a conversation beyond a mutter is forbidden. She winced everytime Dani spoke at normal volume or above during the meal. And the smell, this artificial smell they are pumping through the place, it feels alien, puts her on edge. One year, maybe they will just skip her birthday entirely, stay home, have a takeaway. But, but, but. Etta realised a long time ago that your birthday is not about you, it is about everyone else making themselves feel good. She sees an infinity of celebrations, stretching out until death, doing things she has no real interest in doing, being given gifts she has no use or care for, and there is nothing to do about it. Her therapist says she needs to assert herself more. He says a lot.

She flicks her phone to life on instinct, reaches for Instagram despite there being no signal in this underground bunker, off again. She chooses to ignore Dani's slight frown.

"The waiters are ignoring us."

"Yeah, they are a bit." Dani turns in her chair, looking towards the bar. The bartender is calmly throwing together some complicated drink. Etta wonders how they hold all the recipes in their head, especially in those crowded bars that have music screaming constantly. Unless they tape recipes beneath the counter? That is what she would do.

"Reckon we could ask him?"

"No. He's a bartender. He doesn't do payments."

"Why not? If we were sat at the bar he would. Why can't he do it?"

Dani turns back to her, a scowl settling over her long, thin mouth. "It's not his job. He doesn't work tables."

"But he could work tables."

"He could. He doesn't." Dani is very still. Etta knows not to push when Dani goes still, it means she thinks the conversation does not need continuing. But after a bottle of wine and multiple cocktails, stuck sitting in this hazy grey void, Etta is not feeling very magnanimous. She opens her mouth, feeling fuzz coating her tongue, and prepares to launch into a vague rant about why the bartender absolutely should handle payments when, of course, of course, a waiter pops up out of nowhere. Big smile across his face, thick, like it is painted, something dead about it. Etta is mesmerised.

The waiter slips a leather wallet on the table and rushes away. Etta does not even try to reach for it. She goes back to room watching as Dani meticulously pours over the order, making sure nothing is amiss. A middle-aged couple are enjoying cocktails, sitting directly beneath one of the amber bulbs. The light throws shadows across their animated faces, giving them double chins, extra eyes, shrunken necks. Etta has to stop herself subconsciously picking the fluffy wall beside her beneath the table. It takes her a while before she notices the smoke.

Along the wall, up towards the bar, is a dark wood door. A white *Private* sign on its face almost shines in the gloomy restaurant. Something about it strikes Etta as off. At first she thinks it is just the haziness of the light, but after staring for a while she realises that smoke is coming out from beneath the door. A creeping starts in her stomach, quick and violent.

"Hey," she says quietly. Dani looks up from her calculations and turns to see where Etta is pointing.

"What?"

"Smoke. From the door. See?"

Dani stays turned around for a while. Etta watches the back of her head. She feels as if she is somehow zooming in on the fiercely cropped density of her hair.

"Huh," says Dani, "Yeah. Weird."

"Do you think we should tell someone?"

Dani turns back around but does not look at Etta. She looks down instead, tapping the table rhythmically with the wallet. "I mean, it's probably fine, right? No fire alarm."

The creeping in Etta's stomach is growing. She knows, instinctively, that this is very wrong. Yet she does not do

164

anything. She just keeps sitting, gripping her handbag so tight she can feel the fake leather leaving impressions in palms like a stone carving. The middle aged couple are still here, laughing at some joke, and the other occupied tables seem just as unmoved.

"Hey." Dani is leaning in. She must have been talking.

"What, sorry, what were you saying?"

"I was asking if you wanted to see what was on at the cinema tomorrow. You all right?"

"Yes, no, sorry, I'm... what?"

Dani rolls her eyes. It is a gesture she has perfected over their years together. It makes Etta want to rip a nail out with pliers. She tries to muddle together a coherent thought, find some sense of meaning in what Dani is asking her, but all she can think about is the smoke. It is getting thicker, winding up in lazy tendrils, indisputable now. What colour is it? Hard to tell in this stupid light. Smoke colour means something, doesn't it? White for wood and leaves, black for rubbish, or maybe not, she has no idea. Can she smell it? Maybe, she thinks she can, although that might be in her head. She almost doubts the smoke is there, but Dani saw it too, smoke is coming from the private door.

"We need to tell someone about the smoke."

"Why? I'm sure it's fine, baby."

Etta grips her handbag so tight it hurts. She manages to catch the waiter's eye as he rustles back into the room and waves him over. Dani glares at her before hurriedly turning her gaze back to the bill.

"I'm so sorry, but, but there's smoke, coming from the door. I thought you should know…"

The waiter turns to look towards the little plumes idly puffing out into the room. He looks at it for a long while. Dani is tapping the wallet again, looking at it as if she wants to tear it to pieces. Etta suspects she is not thinking about the wallet.

At last, the waiter turns back and smiles. His teeth are straight. "Don't worry about that, madam. All fine, I assure you. Though I appreciate you pointing it out. I'll grab you the card machine in a moment, thanks so much for waiting." And before Etta can stop him he scuttles off again. His left leg passes through the edge of the smoke and sends it wildly spiralling outwards. By now, a couple of the other patrons have noticed, and are starting to mutter to one another. There is an animal unease taking over the room. Etta believes that there is some great shared mind somehow, when people all instinctively begin to react the same without speaking, and she is quite confident that is happening now. Dani is still looking down. She is tapping the wallet again. Rhythmic. Should Etta stand up? She should stand, that feels like the sensible thing to do. But she is weighed down, her own body works against her. She has never been more conscious of the feeling of a seat. Her legs are leaden. Surely they should leave. But the waiter said it was fine. He seemed so calm and assured, as if this was the most normal thing. Her breath comes quick and sharp like pins.

"We should go," she whispers. Why is she whispering?

166

Dani does not look up. Tap tap tap.

"*Dani -* "

"We can't go," says Dani calmly, "Until we've paid."

Etta leans back in her chair. The smoke is still far down the room but higher now, framing Dani from a distance. Stray tentacles kiss the light fixtures, paw at the bar, scurry across the floorboards. She can definitely smell it now, a woody smoke, the smoke of a campfire or a stove left a little open or the leftovers of fireworks. A comforting smell, elsewhere, no terrible thing. The waiter said it was fine.

"This is ridiculous. We, we don't need to - look, look at it! It's a, a thing, it definitely is something. We can come back and pay another time.

Tap tap tap. "That's illegal. Look, it's fine, we'll just pay. He said he was fetching the card machine."

"Dani," And she stands, propelled up like a rocket, legs almost trembling from the suddenness of it. "We are going home. We can pay another time." She is speaking too loudly. People are looking.

Finally Dani looks up at her, her sharp features cuttings through the gloom. She is speaking louder too, still calm but projecting enough for others to hear. "The waiter said it's fine. We can wait."

Etta looks about, clocking the faces that watch her while trying to avoid eye-contact. "I don't... I don't think..."

"I'm sure it's fine."

"Your friend is right," says the middle aged woman Etta has been watching. The light rips her face up like a Picasso. "If there was a problem, they'd have told us. Once you've settled up, like she says, you can go."

The man with her nods curtly, as if he had said all that. Etta wants to strangle him, but she remains calm. She walks briskly to the stairs that lead up to the outside. One foot rests on the first step, but she does not proceed. She looks back into the room, back to Dani. Some people are still watching, most have returned to their muttered conversations, while her girlfriend is fetching a card from her purse. Her heart hammers. She is not thinking anything, not really, it is a pull of different feelings she cannot quite explain. She has no idea how long she is standing there, one foot up, one down.

She comes back to the table and sits. The smoke keeps on pouring in. Dani flashes her a quick smile before looking back into the restaurant for the waiter. There is nobody about. The bartender has gone.

"Did you enjoy the meal?" she asks.

"Yeah. You asked me that."

"Ah, yeah. Banoffee, right?"

"Banoffee, right." Etta gets her phone out again, no signal underground, pops it away. She cannot think of anything to say. All the words have run out. She watches the smoke increasingly fill the space. She can hear a sound, distant, like a rushing ocean through many walls, or wind on a far hill blowing in and out. It does not matter. They can just pay, and they can go. She looks about for the waiter, but things

168

are getting hazy. She thinks about last Sunday, when Dani came home late from the office and collapsed on the sofa, head in her lap, and immediately fell asleep, and Etta did not wake her but let her sleep, a little drool at the corner of her mouth, still in her shoes and blazer. It had been raining, drops scratching at the windows. The smell of that evening's cooking slowly melting away with the night. The occasional footfall of their upstairs neighbours.

"He'll come with the card machine to us next, right?" She is shocked to hear herself speaking, it almost makes her laugh.

"Course. He said he would. We'll pay and we'll go."

The smoke is curling up over the table, winding around the bowls and empty glasses. A sort of fog is gathering between them. Etta takes off her glasses and wipes them on her skirt, it does not make a difference. Her heartbeat is in her mouth.

"Dani? Dani?

"Don't worry. Someone will come soon. We'll pay up, and we'll go. Somebody will be here soon."

London Independent Story Prize 3rd Round Finalist

Aneeta Sundararaj

Selva

By the time I retrieved the documents from the A3-sized brown envelope, my lawyer, with her burgundy-coloured fingernails, was already back in her seat at the Bar Table on the other side of a low, shellac-painted wooden barricade. The top-most one reinforced the reason I was at High Court 6 (Family Division), Kuala Lumpur. Dated 24 September 2024, my full name – Manickaselva s/o Ambattan – was listed as the Petitioner for this Divorce.

I hadn't expected this. Married and possibly childless, yes. But never divorced. Still, this morning, for the first time in a long while, I'd found something good in the reflection from the bathroom mirror. Staring at the eyes that were similar to my mother's, Appa's bulbous nose and thick, coarse hair, I had smiled.

Appa. My father.

Court clerks exchanged files; lawyers of all shape, genders and ethnicities converged to exchange documents, negotiate deals and/or prepare for their cases; a policeman rubbed his eyes so as to remain awake. I wondered if Appa had the same sense of apprehension the day he went to court some thirty-odd years ago.

***

170

At 6.39 a.m. on 14 February 1993, Ambattan Cinnasamy tugged the collar of his crisp white cotton shirt, arranging it across his shoulders. With one hand, he ran a plastic comb over his salt-and-pepper coloured hair. With the other, he smoothed down errant curls.

"Your hair not only makes you look good," he said to a boy watching him as intently as only an impressionable teenage son in awe of his father can. "It is like a map of your feelings. If it's white, you're stressed. If healthy, it's smooth and shiny. If break-"

"Come. Breakfast," my mother interrupted us.

Appa put down his comb and said, "Let's eat."

Some twenty minutes later, with bellies full of homemade *idly, sambhar* and chutney, we hopped onto his motorcycle and headed for the sundry shop at the entrance of Harvard Estate on the outskirts of town. The land mass of the former rubber plantation spanned ten hectares and was once home to one hundred rubber tappers and their families. When it was sold, seemingly in haste, the transfer papers recorded a single registered owner. Workers like Appa were neither notified of the sale, nor compensated; they were merely issued eviction notices.

With the passage of time, the new owner was desirous of divesting his interest in Harvard Estate. His intention to subdivide the land into one hundred different lots was subverted by bureaucracy. In accordance with piecemeal government policy, the local council deemed that Appa and his former colleagues, by virtue of being Indian and Hindu, were 'not sons of the soil' and couldn't own land in their country of birth. The former rubber tappers of Harvard Estate decided to protest.

It happened in mere seconds. The tractors careened onto the land and headed straight for Appa and his friends. He moved out of the way when the front of the claw was six inches away from him, fell to his side, breaking the impact of the fall by landing on his outstretched hands. The abstract of a police report filed later to support a subsequently unsuccessful claim for damages stated that Appa's suffered from a gash on his forehead and his hands were lacerated.

"Why did this have to happen? What are we going to do now?" My father's lament to my mother a few nights later filtered through the thin walls into my room. I imagined them lying next to each other with my father, holding up his bandaged fingers, knowing that they would never again be nimble enough for a barber to excel at his trade. I fell asleep to the sounds of my parents' soft weeping.

Many years later, when I was interviewed by a newspaper about how I started in the men's grooming industry, I said the following:

> "When I was fourteen, my father recruited me. Every day, after school, while other boys played football or went for tuition classes, I spent time in my father's barber's shop. In the beginning, I only swept the floor and cleaned the brushes with boiling water. Slowly-slowly, I learnt from him. Followed his style. Like this funny thing I must do with the scissors – snip, snip, snip three times before I actually cut the hair. If I don't do this, I don't know why, I cannot cut the hair."

What I didn't tell the reporter was that for two years after Appa's accident, and a much-reduced income, I saw the light go out in my father's eyes and watched him limp from customer to customer. Often, he'd say, "We shouldn't have fought."

***

I looked around the auditorium of University Kebangsaan in Kuala Lumpur. The only seat available was one in the third row, right in the middle – the worst possible seat. I wished I could tell what the lecture had been about, but I spent most of my time mired in the shame of arriving late for this, an introduction to a degree in Bachelor of Business Administration. An hour later, I walked out into the bright sunshine only to bump into a girl.

"Are you okay?" It wasn't the words she said. It wasn't her hand on mine. It wasn't her smile. It was her voice. There was concern in it. So unaccustomed was I to such a show of emotion that I was instantly drawn to it.

As was the case with every romance, we proceeded along a well-plotted route from 'study together,' and 'dating' to 'meeting the parents' and 'getting engaged.'

"We will build our business from scratch," she said when we set the wedding date.

"We will have the best brand for men's hair care and grooming services," she said when we returned from the jewellers.

"Together, we will never fail. We are a team," she said on the eve of our wedding.

It was as though my dreams had become her dreams.

Nevertheless...

Each time I returned her rictus grin with a wide smile, I pondered the orderliness of my past and the complete uncertainty of my future.

In those early days of our marriage and setting up our flagship salon in Bangsar, where I catered to cutting hair, shaving and grooming our clients, Hema dealt with the marketing and branding of our business. She would stand by the main door and hand out booklets. "Marketing materials," she called them. I was stunned by the amount of research she'd done when I read the Introduction she'd written:

> 'Here at SuperSalons, we believe that our hair is an extension of our being. It is the conduit that connects us to the universe and our soul. Therefore, our highly trained stylists won't only style your hair. The hair care rituals we recommend and practice are tailored and personalised to suit your individual needs.'

With all her effort, SuperSalons was turning a profit in less than a year. Firmly on the proverbial ladder of success, we paid off the business loan in the next two years and she began to prepare a business plan for the expansion of our business and, in her words, "global domination."

***

One day, some five years into our marriage, she flung open the door to my study in the condominium unit we bought above our salon.

"Guess what?" She held her iPhone, a new status-conscious acquisition.

I jerked my chin forward, as if to say, "What?"

"I've been chosen. My friend, you know, Shobi? The financial planner I want to ask for help. She nominated me."

"For?"

"I am the next Vice President of Fortune Wheels." Within two years of setting up our business, Hema had become a staunch member of this organisation that supported women entrepreneurs.

I leapt out of my chair to hug her, mighty proud of my wife. She didn't fling her arms around my neck, but put her palms up, as though to push me away. Surprised, I backed away from her, uncertain of what had changed between us. Nonetheless, I heard her mumble, as she walked out of the room, "Because of me, only, SuperSalons is a success."

While life seemingly carried on as normal, we no longer made eye contact.

***

I held a razor to my cheek just as Hema walked into the ensuite master bathroom. In an hour, we were to meet with the local bank to submit the business plan for the fourth branch of SuperSalons. Looking at my reflection, she'd giggled. Where were all the 'hello darling,' 'sweetie-pie,' and 'babe,' of when we were first married?

I frowned. "What?"

"Nothing."

I put the razor down, turned to her and said, "What is it? What is the problem now?"

"You have to bend to shave."

I frowned. "What?"

"See." She pinched my waist. "Fatty bom-bom."

"Oh…" I sucked in my stomach, reached for the bath towel and threw it across my torso. I prayed I appeared nonchalant.

"You look so old. Like fifty years old."

I picked up the razor and continued to shave.

'I'm only thirty-five, for fuck's sake,' I wanted to shout. Instead, I swallowed both my hurt and plans for a romantic dinner over the weekend. When I walked into our bedroom five minutes later, I accepted Hema's gift of a gym membership, instead.

***

Legs, hip-width apart.

Bend at the hips.

Knees bent.

Lift barbell.

Place barbell onto shoulders.

Inhale. Squat.

Exhale. Rise.

Repeat.

The meditative rhythm of this exercise forced me to block the destructive and divergent thoughts clogging my mind. And, whenever I grunted, it was as though I was expelling a build-up of angst and sheer frustration.

Was this because of…

Bullshit!

I dropped the weight to the floor.

"Hey!" The only other gym member during this ungodly hour before the sun rose completely shouted.

"Sorry," I mumbled, also apologetic for I was now swearing more than ever. I picked up my towel, wiped the sweat off my brow and walked to the lockers. I needed to do something to get all these feelings out.

Once inside the car, I switched on the radio. The news was full of a dreaded virus that had the potential of ravaging the world. It had been given a name: Covid-19. I turned into Starbucks, parked the car, walked into the airconditioned building and broke the most basic rule of a post-workout rule – I ordered a breakfast full of carbs and a hazelnut coffee. Once I was settled in one corner of the café, I opened up my laptop and started typing a letter to Shobi. It was the only way I could think of to tell my side of the story.

Starbucks, Petaling Jaya

18 February 2020

My Shobi. My Darling.

There will be no order to what I write.

I wish I could say that I felt an instant spark when we first met. Nothing of the sort. I was your friend because you were Hema's friend. Pure friend zone status. I mean, all the meetings to discuss the finances were at our salon. Not once did we go to your office. Until that fateful day. I often wonder if anything would have happened between us if I, and not Hema, as usual, brought our files to you.

"Shall we have coffee?" Your question was so sudden I was taken aback. I couldn't say a word and merely nodded. It became worse when you asked if I wanted milk and sugar. It took all of me to hold up two fingers. That was the best I could do.

You smiled, My Shobi. At me. No woman had ever smiled at me in that way before. Not even Hema.

I am not sure what prompted you to say, "We should perhaps…"

If my shock wasn't apparent when I first walked into your office to find how cosy it was, it must have been after you pressed a button and the doors slid open.

"This is a SOHO, darling!" I heard the laughter in your words. "Small Office Home Office. Home always has a bedroom nearby, no?"

"Oh…"

Like an automaton, I let you take my hand and lead me to the room. I wanted to ask if you were going to seduce me. I wanted to know if there were things I should be careful of. I wanted to know how to hold you. I wanted to…

I should have said 'what now?' when we sat down.

But no words came out. Instead, we stared at each other. Then...

How do I write the words?

Should I?

I must, if only to process my thoughts. Let me try...

With central and silent air-conditioning, there was none of the usual relief of removing my clothes because of the sticky feeling on the skin from our tropical heat. The sheets weren't rough, but soft to the touch, with the scent of jasmine in the air. The scene seemed to be set for seduction.

When we 'merged' (I can't think of a better word), it was as though, having been separated all our lives, I had come home. I remember nothing more after that except a sense of surety and familiarity. I understood the meaning of making love and not merely being allowed to have sex. I wanted to weep from the emotions coursing through my body. I did try to explain it to you when we later lay on damp sheets. But it all came out wrong and twisted.

"I feel so..."

"What?"

I wanted to say 'alive'. Instead, in those moments when I hesitated, all the thoughts that we may have done something wrong crept into my mind. So, I did the only thing I've ever known.

"Come," I said while rising to my feet. "Let's get back to work." I walked out into the office area and made a bee line for the kitchenette. I busied myself trying to make a drink. Coffee. Tea. Something.

You came up behind me, fully dressed.

"Stop." There was much kindness in your voice. "You go sit down. Look over the papers. I'll do this."

For the next ten minutes, I tried hard to focus on the paper work. I couldn't remember a word I read then. I can't remember a word of it now. But I do remember this next bit in minute detail.

You walked over to the tiny table for two. You put a plate in front of me. In that short space of time, you understood my need and made a simple meal of toast with scrambled eggs.

No one will ever know that when I left your SOHO, I sat in the car park for what seemed like hours. And I wept. For my feelings. For the joy I felt in your arms. For the wrong I'd done my wife. Most of all, I wept because for the first time in my life, I knew that I wanted something more than what I have.

That's it, My Shobi. My Darling.

No.

My Love.

Your Selva

I left Starbucks that day with this letter in my laptop. As I took that first step back into the real world, I knew that ghosting her from now on would hurt Shobi no end. It would hurt me even more.

***

The memory of those few hours with My Shobi stayed with me, sometimes bright as a spark, and sometimes as sharp as dust in the eye. There were times, though, when I simply couldn't avoid speaking with her, especially when we discussed business matters. Like the time the Movement Control Order imposed by the government to curtail the spread of the deadly disease was catastrophic for the business. All the money we'd pooled together to expand our business went down the drain. Even though the number of staff was now down to two, there were still utilities and other bills to pay. I always kept our conversations professional, but I wanted nothing more than to eliminate, altogether, the chasm between us.

When I entered the flat the day the Movement Control Order was lifted on 1 November 2021, Hema was still awake and in the kitchen. If I had to put words to it, I'd say that there was relief in the air. After all, we'd survived by keeping our flagship salon and letting the rest go. With this possible reboot of our business, it was a time to celebrate. I'd avoided Shobi for more than a year now. I'd avoided my wife. This was my chance.

It had been so long…

I didn't give her time to protest. Instead, when I grabbed her arm and led her in the direction of our bedroom, I heard her gasp and the metal spatula fall onto the kitchen countertop. The silence filled my body, making me aware of every single inhalation and exhalation. In mere moments, her heart pounded fast and hard against my chest. I refocused, trying to make our rhythms match. When she spoke – "Hurry up," – the only person I wanted to be with in that moment was My Shobi. I rolled off Hema and lay on my back. She snorted derisively. I knew it: in my wife's eyes, I wasn't merely a failure as a businessman, I was now a complete failure as a man.

***

'You are not responsible for someone else's bad behaviour.'

It was the mantra I recited from the last night Hema and I were ever intimate close to three years ago, now. Each time I said it to my reflection in the mirror, my shoulders became that much straighter, I lifted my chin that bit higher and I inhaled deeply. +

When the courtroom door opened, signalling the arrival of the judge, I turned to My Shobi smiling wide and bright.

"Are parties in agreement?" The judge's voice boomed throughout the court.

I smiled back. It was time to live my best life, divorced or not.

Biographies

Alice Frecknall is a writer and fine artist. Her debut poetry collection, Somewhere Something is Burning, is published by Out-Spoken Press. Her writing is widely anthologised, including in The London Magazine, The Stinging Fly, and fourteen poems, and shortlisted for The London Magazine Poetry Prize 2023 and Out-Spoken Prize for Poetry 2023.

Han Smith is a queer writer, translator and community literacy teacher, and received a London Writers Award in 2019/2020. Han's work has been published and commissioned by Lunate, Cipher Press, Five Dials, Litro, The Interpreter's House and the European Poetry Festival, and shortlisted/longlisted for prizes including the Desperate Literature Prize, the VS Pritchett Award, the Bridport Prize and the Brick Lane Bookshop Prize. Her debut novel was published by John Murray Originals in June 2024: Portraits at the Palace of Creativity and Wrecking.

Mary Ethna Black is a globetrotting doctor from Northern Ireland, represented by Emma Bal at Madeleine Milburn Agency. Prizes include the Irish Writers Centre Novel Fair, Fish short memoir, London Independent Story, Globe Soup short story and Letterkenny Flash fiction. Abacus will publish her memoir, 'Splav — Adventures with my family on the River Sava' in summer 2026. Set in

Serbia, this is a love story about finding home in an unstable world. Welcome to catfish, coffee, and chaos.

Fiona Dignan started writing during lockdown to cope with the chaos of home-schooling her four children. Her work has been published in various anthologies and magazines including Mslexia, Pop Shot and WestWord. She has won the London Society Poetry Prize (2023), The Plaza Prize for Sudden Fiction (2023) and the Farnham Flash Fiction competition (2024). She has been listed for the Bath Short Story Prize and the London Independent Story Prize. In 2023 she was nominated for the Pushcart Prize.

Katy Severson is a London-based writer and chef with an unending passion for food and nature. Her work has appeared in SLOP Magazine, Bon Appetit, HuffPost and Atrium Poetry among others. She is also the editor-in-chief of Companion magazine, a biannual print publication from GAIL's.

Tracy Fahey is an award-winning Irish author of six books. She has been a British Fantasy Award finalist in 2017, 2022, and 2024. In 2024, she won the Paul Cave Prize for Literature. She was granted a Saari Fellowship for 2023 by the Kone Foundation. Fahey's short fiction has appeared in more than 40 anthologies. Her writing is supported by residencies in Ireland, Scotland, Greece and Finland.

Rosie Parry lives and works in London. She studied Creative Writing at Goldsmiths.

Samuel Prince's debut poetry collection, 'Ulterior Atmospheres', was published in 2020 by Live Canon. His work has more recently appeared in The Plaza Prizes Anthology 2, pioneertown, Rust & Moth and Willawaw

Journal. He lives in Norfolk. More information can be found at www.samuelprince.co.uk

Georgia lives in the Cotswolds. Her work has featured in Shooter, Northern Gravy, on BBC Radio, and at Cheltenham Literature Festival. She's won commendations from the Wells and Sean O'Faolain Prizes, and been shortlisted for the Alpine Prize, and Laurie Lee Prize. In 2024, she won the Scratch Books competition.

Patrick Cash is a British-Irish writer living in London. He was a winner of the Felicity Bryan New Voices 2024 and Hachette UK Grow Your Story competitions for his work-in-progress novel, Fireworks. His short fiction has won a Creative Future Award, and been published in The London Magazine and Fictionable.

Tony Warner lives in a churchyard just outside Norwich, where he is renovating a 13th century church tower for use as his scriptorium. He is the author of four novels and book of short stories. www.tonywarner47.com

Jean Roarty lives in Dublin, Ireland. She has had stories published in anthologies including Southword 38 New International Writing and, most recently, in the Melbourne based MSB forthcoming anthology Light and Shadow. She enjoys sport and travel.

Anne Wilkins is a sleep-deprived teacher in New Zealand who writes in her spare time. Her love of writing is fuelled by copious amounts of coffee, reading and hope. Her work can be found in Apex Magazine, Cosmic Horror Monthly, Elegant Literature, Sci-Fi Shorts and elsewhere. Visit: www.annewilkinsauthor.com

Erini Loucaides is an Australian-Cypriot writer and English teacher with a BA in English from the University of London. She is an Oxbelly Writing Retreat Fellow and a Commonwealth Foundation Mentorship Recipient. Her work has been featured in Mslexia Best Women's Fiction (twice) and the Bournemouth Anthology amongst other publications.

Sophia Skyers is a second generation Jamaican from the Midlands, and lives in London. She was Top Tier Globe Soup Finalist in its 2023 Short Story Competition, and has published flash fiction pieces in Flash Flood. She has a PhD in Geography and writes about people and place.

Joe Wedgbury is a writer of short fiction and poetry. His work has been featured in South Bank Poetry, Bristol 24/7, Blood Orange and Milk. He received the Bristol Short Story Prize Sansom Award in 2020.

Koushik Banerjea is the author of two novels, 'Another Kind of Concrete' (2020) and 'Category Unknown' (2022). His short stories have appeared in various magazines and anthologies, including Aeos, Verbal, and FeignLit. He has been a carer, youth worker, and journalist. The common thread though has always been telling tales, tall or otherwise. He lives in London.

Perdita lives on Dartmoor with her husband and two daughters. She spends her time writing, teaching, and preventing the toddler from putting small, dangerous objects up the baby's nose. Her latest short story, Old Bones, was awarded second place in the 2024 Writers and Artists Short Story Competition.

Helen Kennedy is a writer of short stories and flash fiction published by Fly on the Wall Press, The Bristol Prize, Brick Lane Bookshop Prize, Flash 500, the Oxford Flash Fiction Prize and NFFD anthology. She has recently competed a debut novel 'Blessed Women,' for which she is seeking representation and is currently writing another about fertility and Irish folklore.

Charlie Kite is a poet and short fiction author, focusing on nature in the modern world, magical realism, and individuals and communities in change. He graduated with a Creative Writing Degree from Oxford, and currently lives in Hastings. He's currently working on a novel.

Aneeta Sundararaj is an award-winning short story writer whose stories are included in a collection called 'Tapestry of the Mind and Other Stories' (Penguin Random House SEA, 2024). Her novel, 'The Age of Smiling Secrets' was shortlisted for the Book Award 2020 in Malaysia. In 2021, Aneeta successfully completed a doctoral thesis called 'Management of Prosperity Among Artistes in Malaysia'. To know more, please visit http://www.howtotellagreatstory.com and http://www.aneetasundararaj.com